PUFFIN BOOKS

# TOO SMALL TO FAIL

Morris Gleitzman grew up in England and went to live in Australia when he was sixteen. He worked as a frozen-chicken thawer, sugar-mill rolling-stock unhooker, fashion-industry trainee, department-store Santa, TV producer, newspaper columnist and screenwriter. Then he had a wonderful experience. He wrote a novel for young people. Now he's one of the bestselling children's authors in Australia. He lives in Melbourne, but visits Britain regularly. His many books include *Two Weeks with the Queen*, *Water Wings*, *Bumface*, *Boy Overboard* and *Once*.

Visit Morris at his website:
www.morrisgleitzman.com

Also by Morris Gleitzman

# TOO SMALL TO FAIL

## MORRIS GLEITZMAN

PUFFIN

PUFFIN BOOKS

Published by the Penguin Group
Penguin Books Ltd, 80 Strand, London WC2R 0RL, England
Penguin Group (USA) Inc., 375 Hudson Street, New York, New York 10014, USA
Penguin Group (Canada), 90 Eglinton Avenue East, Suite 700, Toronto, Ontario, Canada M4P 2Y3
(a division of Pearson Penguin Canada Inc.)
Penguin Ireland, 25 St Stephen's Green, Dublin 2, Ireland (a division of Penguin Books Ltd)
Penguin Group (Australia), 250 Camberwell Road, Camberwell, Victoria 3124, Australia
(a division of Pearson Australia Group Pty Ltd)
Penguin Books India Pvt Ltd, 11 Community Centre, Panchsheel Park,
New Delhi – 110 017, India
Penguin Group (NZ), 67 Apollo Drive, Rosedale, Auckland 0632, New Zealand
(a division of Pearson New Zealand Ltd)
Penguin Books (South Africa) (Pty) Ltd, 24 Sturdee Avenue, Rosebank, Johannesburg 2196,
South Africa

Penguin Books Ltd, Registered Offices: 80 Strand, London WC2R 0RL, England

puffinbooks.com

First published in Australia by Penguin Group (Australia),
a division of Pearson Group Australia Pty Ltd 2011
First published in Great Britain by Puffin Books 2011
001 – 10 9 8 7 6 5 4 3 2 1

Copyright © Creative Input Pty, 2011
All rights reserved

The moral right of the author has been asserted

Set in Minion
Printed in Great Britain by Clays Ltd, St Ives plc

British Library Cataloguing in Publication Data
A CIP catalogue record for this book is available from the British Library

ISBN: 978–0–241–95520–8

*For Mary-Anne*

Oliver wanted more.

Not squillions of dollars and private jets and solid gold zips on his school bag. Not even his own paint-ball island in the Pacific or lolly trucks backing up to his place every day.

Just more than this.

More than standing in a crowded shopping centre trying to have a friendship with a dog through a pet-shop window.

What Oliver wanted was a black-and-white streak hurtling towards him across a park and yelping with joy and leaping onto his chest and wagging mud all over him and making his face wet with love.

The dog in the pet shop wanted that too, Oliver could see. It was gazing up at him, puddle eyes eager and hopeful, quivering nose making smears on the glass as it tried to snuffle him.

Oliver sighed.

He'd been trying to explain for days how things were, and the dog still didn't understand.

Oliver leaned closer to the window and tried again.

'I can't take you home,' he said sadly to the dog. 'We just have to be friends through the glass.'

The dog's whole body was quivering like it did every time they met. The strands of newspaper dangling from its ears were jiggling and wobbling with excitement.

Oliver could see the dog still didn't get it.

He knew why.

You couldn't be real friends through glass. Not when one of you was a dog.

This is hopeless, thought Oliver. I'm not being fair. I'm just hurting us both.

He had another thought.

Maybe they had to stop meeting like this.

Oliver didn't want to. He loved coming here. At school it was all he could think of, even in art. And anyway, how could you explain to a friend that it was all over when you weren't even allowed into the pet shop because the manager reckoned you were a time-waster and a pest?

Oliver sighed again.

'Nice puppy that,' said a voice.

At first Oliver thought the person standing next to him was a kid. She was only a bit taller than him and her hair was in a ponytail. Then he saw her grown-up hands.

'Yes,' said Oliver. 'It is.'

He didn't know how the woman could see the dog properly with her sunglasses on.

'I think I'll buy it,' said the woman.

She went into the shop.

Oliver wanted to tell her it was too late. He wanted to yell out that the dog was already sold to a loving owner. But he couldn't because it wasn't.

He watched the woman go up to an assistant and point to the dog. The assistant came over and lifted the dog out of the window. The dog looked at Oliver and then at the woman and then back at Oliver.

Suddenly Oliver remembered what Dad always said.

Take a chance.

Have a punt.

Risk it.

Oliver picked up his school bag and hurried into the shop. As soon as he was inside, the manager yelled at him.

'Oi, you. I've told you. Out.'

The manager was a big scary man with poodle hair. But Oliver was too frantic to feel scared. He had to move fast. The assistant was handing the woman a piece of paper and explaining about dog injections.

Oliver realised he didn't have a plan. Dad would never take a punt without a plan.

Too late.

Oliver struggled to think of something to say.

He could offer to pay a hundred dollars more than the woman. Then ask if the dog could live in the shop for a few years. Just until the manager realised working with animals made him grumpy, and he retired and Oliver got a loan and bought the shop.

Trouble was, the manager looked too grumpy now to even appreciate such a good offer.

Oliver took a deep breath of budgie-scented air to try to calm his thoughts.

A better idea hit him.

I'll ask the woman if I can come to her place sometimes to visit the dog, he said to himself.

She might agree, specially if he offered to get the dog hairs off her sofa with sticky tape.

Then Oliver noticed the woman's grubby jeans and dusty boots and the bits of straw stuck to her jacket.

This wasn't good.

If she was a farmer he'd never be able to get to her place. Farms were hundreds of kilometres away.

'Are you deaf?' the manager was saying to Oliver. 'Get lost.'

Oliver wondered if the woman had Skype on her farm. That could work.

Unless she told him to get lost as well.

The assistant handed the dog to the woman and said she'd get her a dog box from out the back.

'No need,' said the woman. 'I'm hoping this young bloke will give me a hand.'

Oliver realised she meant him.

The woman was smiling at him. For a moment there was something about her smile that was sort of familiar, but Oliver couldn't place it.

He stared at the woman, wondering if she was joking. It was hard to tell with her sunglasses on. The manager and the assistant looked like they definitely thought she was joking.

But when the woman put the dog into Oliver's arms, he realised she wasn't.

# 2

'This way.'

The woman led Oliver down an escalator.

Oliver tried not to think about where they were going, or about having to give the dog back when they got there. He just wanted to enjoy the warm panting wagging bundle in his arms.

Up close the dog's puddle eyes were even more eager and hopeful. And its fur was short and incredibly soft. It felt like velvet curtains. Or what Oliver imagined velvet curtains would feel like if Mum and Dad had them instead of stainless-steel designer blinds.

At the bottom of the escalator, Oliver briefly wondered why the woman had asked him to do this. She was carrying his school bag, which was about six times heavier than the dog.

But then the dog licked him on the nose, which felt so good he forgot the question.

The woman was striding across an underground

car park. Oliver followed.

He hoped her car was a long way away. Perhaps with her sunglasses on she wouldn't even be able to find it.

'If you were mine,' said Oliver to the dog, 'I'd call you Barclay. That's what Mum and Dad were going to call my little brother or sister if I ever had one. It's the name of a really big bank overseas.'

Oliver could tell the dog liked the name.

A lot.

Oliver sighed. He was being thoughtless again.

'Sorry,' he said. 'I didn't mean to get your hopes up. I'm not allowed to have a pet. My parents are too rich.'

The dog looked puzzled.

'Being rich is a really full-time job,' explained Oliver. 'Mum and Dad work incredibly hard and they're too busy for pets.'

The dog looked like it didn't understand how anybody could be too busy for pets.

'It's complicated,' said Oliver. 'You'd understand if you met them.'

The woman's car was a long way off, over in a corner away from all the other cars, but finally they got there.

It was a battered ute.

'Hop in,' said the woman, smiling in a friendly way.

Oliver hesitated. He was ten. People had told him he should be careful of strangers and cars until he was at least thirty.

'Is somebody waiting for you?' said the woman.

'Yes,' said Oliver. 'Our housekeeper, Vickey. I'm meeting her outside the supermarket.'

'This won't take long, I promise,' said the woman. 'I just need your help for a sec. Get in.'

Oliver decided to take a punt. The woman probably needed help giving the dog some car training. So it wouldn't be naughty on the way home and she wouldn't have to try to get a lead round its neck and teach it discipline while she was driving.

'OK,' he said.

Anything, if it meant he could hang on to Barclay for a bit longer.

As Oliver climbed into the passenger seat, he had a hopeful thought. Maybe the woman wasn't a farmer after all. Maybe she was just a keen gardener with a house not too far away. And she'd have to say yes to him visiting after this.

The woman got in the driver's side and locked the doors.

Oliver was surprised.

Then he realised why she'd done it.

'Don't worry,' he whispered to Barclay. 'It's so you can't run off.'

'This'll only take a couple of minutes, Oliver,' said the woman. 'Vickey won't mind. Housekeepers are used to waiting.'

Oliver looked at her.

How did she know his name?

Maybe he'd mentioned it when he was chatting to Barclay on the escalator. Funny, though, he didn't remember doing that.

'You must really love that dog,' said the woman. 'Coming here every day after school.'

Oliver nodded.

But his mind was racing.

Had the woman been spying on him?

Then Oliver saw something on the seat between them. Something that gleamed softly in the murky car-park lights.

A kitchen knife.

A big one.

It was a bit rusty, but it looked sharp.

Oliver stared at it. He had a scary thought.

Dad had told him once how the kids of rich bankers sometimes got kidnapped and their parents had to pay millions to get them back. Mum told Dad to stop being over-dramatic. But Oliver looked it up on Google. Sometimes the parents were sent bits of their kids in the post. Not just fingernail clippings, bigger bits.

Oliver tried to stay calm. As far as he knew, things like that didn't happen in Australia. Only in unlawful places like South America and New Zealand.

But as Oliver hugged Barclay, he couldn't help giving the woman a nervous glance. And then another one.

'You don't know who I am, do you?' said the woman.

Oliver shook his head.

The woman took off her sunglasses.

'Remember me now?' she said.

Oliver stared at her.

'Nancy,' said the woman.

Oliver stared some more. She definitely looked familiar.

Sort of.

'I took care of you,' said Nancy. 'When you were four.'

Oliver remembered.

Kind of.

That was the trouble with having a mother who was always sacking housekeepers. When you'd had nineteen in your life, it put a real strain on your memory.

'Hi, Nancy,' he said, to be polite.

It was a relief knowing who she was. The knife on the seat must just be for peeling fruit or something.

Nancy didn't say hi back. She looked at Oliver for a moment, then stared grimly at the steering wheel and didn't say anything.

Oliver was puzzled. If he was the new owner of the best dog in the world, he'd be feeling a lot happier than she was looking.

'Oliver,' said Nancy, turning back to him. 'Do you know what an investment is?'

Of course I do, thought Oliver. My parents own a bank.

He wanted to ask Nancy if she knew what scissors were, because if she was planning to cut the plastic ID tag off Barclay's paw with that knife she should probably think again.

'Answer me,' said Nancy.

'Yes, I do know,' said Oliver. 'An investment is when you give your money to somebody else for a while. Later they give it back to you with extra money to say thank you.'

Nancy gave a bitter laugh.

Oliver's insides twitched anxiously. People who were feeling bitter shouldn't be planning to do fiddly things with big knives.

'Good answer,' said Nancy.

'Thanks,' said Oliver.

He wondered why, if she thought it was so good, she was still sounding bitter.

'Getting your money back is what should happen,' said Nancy. 'But some people don't keep their promises. A few years ago, when I was your housekeeper, I gave your parents eleven thousand dollars to invest for me. When I asked for it back last month, their office said it was lost.'

Oliver stared at her.

That wasn't possible. That must be a mistake. Mum and Dad were very careful with money. They ran one of the most trusted investment banks in Australia. Dad was always saying so.

'That money was my life savings,' said Nancy. 'I need it back.'

11

Her voice had gone quiet, like grown-ups' voices did when they really meant what they were saying and they were getting upset.

'It's probably just a mistake,' said Oliver. 'I bet Mum and Dad haven't really lost it. They're very good at maths.'

Barclay licked Oliver's chin to show he agreed it was probably just a mistake.

Nancy leaned over and grabbed Oliver's arm. Tight. Her fingers dug into his armpit. Usually that tickled, but not the way she was doing it.

'My family needs that money, Oliver,' she said. 'You're our last hope. Your parents promised it'd be a safe investment. Now they won't even speak to me. And the other mongrels at the bank just keep making excuses.'

Oliver was starting to feel a bit panicky.

He took a deep breath and realised what must have happened. Mum and Dad were always so busy at work, and so stressed, that the staff didn't like to bother them.

But what did Nancy mean, he was her family's last hope?

Of course.

His savings account.

Oliver tried to remember how much was in it. Nine hundred and something dollars. Which was nowhere near eleven thousand. To be a last hope he'd need about nine thousand more. Or maybe ten thousand . . . it was really hard doing maths when somebody was digging their fingers into your armpit.

Oliver stopped trying.

Another strange thing was happening.

Nancy was writing a number on his hand.

'My mobile,' she said. 'So you can let me know how you're going with it.'

'With what?' said Oliver.

'Telling your parents to give me my money back,' said Nancy. 'They'll listen to you. When you ask for something, you always get it, right?'

Oliver hesitated.

That was only partly true. He usually did, but not always. Not pets, for example.

He gave Barclay a sad little squeeze.

Nancy gave his arm a big, painful one.

'I want you to ask them really hard,' she said. 'Really, really hard.'

Her voice was starting to sound scary.

'I'll try,' said Oliver. 'But Mum and Dad are incredibly stressed and busy, so it might take a bit of time.'

Nancy scowled, and Oliver could see that she was feeling very stressed herself.

'A week,' she said. 'That's all I've got.'

'I'll try,' said Oliver again. 'But they don't always listen to me.'

'I'm counting on you,' said Nancy. 'And I'm not the only one who is.'

She let go of his arm and took Barclay from him.

She sat Barclay on her lap. Barclay waited patiently, looking at Oliver.

Nancy picked up the knife and held the blade near Barclay's throat.

'It wouldn't just be me you'd be letting down,' she said.

Oliver stared at her.

He felt sick.

Her hands.

Why hadn't he noticed before? They were covered with scratches and scrapes and bruises.

Violent hands.

Cruel hands.

Hands that wouldn't think twice about killing a dog.

# 3

Oliver sprinted along the crowded city street, trying not to bash into anyone.

Why did everyone have to walk so slowly?

It was alright for them, strolling along and chatting. But some people only had six days, twenty-three hours and, um, however many minutes to save a dog's life.

Oliver was starting to gasp for breath.

He looked around, trying to spot where Vickey was in the car. He couldn't even see her. The traffic still wasn't moving. He'd done the right thing, getting out of the car and going ahead on foot.

He kept running.

Soon Mum and Dad's bank building loomed ahead.

The sight of it made Oliver feel a bit less sick and anxious. He was glad Mum and Dad's bank wasn't an ordinary one. A street level one with grubby carpets and finger-smeared ATMs and those bits of string without pens on them and suspicious characters in motorbike helmets lurking around outside.

A bank on the eighteenth floor of a big tall important building like this one was much safer.

For money and dogs.

Oliver hurried through the gold-framed sliding doors and told the security man who he wanted to see. Then he sat on the squeaky leather sofa and waited for somebody to come down and collect him.

He felt better now he was here.

Mum and Dad would make everything OK. They were upstairs now, doing very fast things with numbers and earning heaps of money.

Making big bikkies, that's what Dad called it. Big bikkies meant millions of dollars, so how could a measly eleven thousand dollars be a problem?

Eleven thousand was little bikkies.

The important thing, Oliver reminded himself, was to keep Mum and Dad calm. He mustn't get them worked up. If Dad heard an investor was threatening a dog with a knife, he'd probably get police snipers involved very fast.

Oliver imagined Nancy and Barclay in a hail of bullets and started to feel sick and anxious again.

The lift door opened and Dad strode out.

'Ollie, what a nice surprise.'

'Hi, Dad,' said Oliver.

'What's wrong? said Dad. 'You look stressed.'

Oliver opened his mouth to ask Dad about Nancy's money. But Dad didn't give him a chance.

'Maths test today, huh?'

Oliver stared blankly at Dad.

Then he remembered the maths test at school. It had been first thing after lunch. Which felt like weeks ago.

'What did you get?' said Dad.

'Seven out of twenty,' said Oliver in a small voice.

He saw Dad give a sigh, and try to hide it with a sympathetic nod.

'Bad luck,' said Dad.

Oliver wished Dad wouldn't keep saying that each time he had a maths test. It wasn't bad luck. He was just hopeless at maths.

'That's not why I'm here, Dad,' said Oliver.

Dad wasn't listening, he was flicking through messages on his phone.

'Come and say a quick hi to Mum,' he said, steering Oliver towards the lift without looking up from the screen.

Oliver got ready to grab his chance in the lift, because once they were upstairs he knew Dad would be too busy. No problem, eighteen floors was plenty of time to ask Dad about Nancy's money, and for Dad to chuckle and explain it was OK, the money wasn't really lost.

They stepped into the lift.

'Dad,' said Oliver as they started to go up.

Dad's phone rang.

Oliver tried to stay calm. Dad must be the only person in the world whose phone worked in a lift.

Above the lift door, numbers were flickering. Oliver stared up at them. He only had fifteen floors left. Or fourteen, or . . . he couldn't work it out. Not when he was stressed.

'Yes to ten million,' said Dad into the phone. 'Yes to sixty-two basis points. Seventy-four mill? He's dreaming.'

He hung up.

'Dad,' said Oliver.

'I love lifts,' said Dad. He was looking up at the numbers too. 'They make me feel like an asset-backed derivative starting off at one dollar and going all the way up to eighteen dollars.'

Normally Oliver would have asked Dad what an asset-backed derivative was, but not now. He only had one floor left.

'Dad,' said Oliver. 'Nancy who used to be our housekeeper thinks you've lost her money.'

The lift came to a stop.

Dad stared at Oliver, frowning.

'Clients shouldn't be pestering you, Ollie,' he said. 'Where did you see her?'

Oliver started to explain how each day after school he spent time in the shopping centre while Vickey was in the supermarket.

Dad's phone beeped.

'Walk and talk, Ollie,' he said, steering Oliver out of the lift.

Before Oliver could tell Dad about Barclay, they were past the reception desk and outside the trading room.

Oliver knew he had no chance now. The trading room was big, almost as big as the living room at home, and full of computer screens and maths geniuses wearing Bluetooth headsets, most of them wanting to ask Dad things.

But today Dad paused before he went in.

'Listen, Ollie,' he said. 'Customers come to us because we're smart and we make more money for them than regular banks. But if people want big bikkies, they've got to understand there's risk. Some investments turn to poo. That's just how it is.'

Oliver couldn't believe what he was hearing. Dad often talked about big bikkies, but he'd never mentioned anything about poo.

'Mum'll explain more,' said Dad, and went off with a man who'd been yelling 'Tokyo' at him.

Oliver stood there, stunned.

It must be true.

Mum and Dad had lost Nancy's money.

Oliver felt cold panic rising inside him. He hurried over to Mum's office, trying not to think how Barclay must be feeling.

Mum was having a meeting with a couple of people. When she saw Oliver she signalled to him to wait. After a couple of minutes she came out.

'Love,' she said. 'What are you doing here? Where's Vickey?'

'In a traffic jam,' said Oliver. 'It's not her fault.'

'Are you OK?' said Mum. 'Is it the maths test?'

Oliver shook his head.

'Something else,' he said. 'Remember Nancy from when I was little? She was at the shopping centre today and she's really upset about you losing her money.'

Mum stared at him.

'Nancy?' she said. 'Housekeeper Nancy?'

Oliver nodded.

'I don't get it,' he said. 'I thought you and Dad were really clever with money.'

Mum sighed.

'We are, love,' she said. 'This doesn't happen often. Well, it didn't use to.'

She turned to a man at a nearby desk, who Oliver remembered was her assistant.

'Hayden,' said Mum. 'Could you check our client list for a Nancy Turner. See if she's one of the . . . you know.'

'Difficult ones,' muttered Hayden.

'I don't like that expression,' said Mum.

Oliver hesitated. He didn't want to take sides against Mum, but this was urgent.

'I think Hayden might be right about Nancy being difficult,' said Oliver.

'How do you mean?' said Mum.

'If she doesn't get her money back,' said Oliver,

'she's going to do something to her dog.'

Mum looked puzzled.

'Do something?' she said. 'What sort of thing?'

'Kill him,' said Oliver.

Mum blinked.

'Did she actually say that?' said Mum.

'No,' said Oliver. 'She didn't actually say it out loud. But . . .'

'But you thought it,' said Mum gently.

Oliver nodded.

Mum gave his shoulders a weary squeeze.

'Love,' she said. 'Do you think you might be watching too many scary movies?'

Her mobile beeped and she glanced at the screen, then looked back at Oliver.

'An investor wouldn't do a thing like that,' she said. 'Not even an upset one. You've got an amazing imagination, Oliver, and a good heart. Just try and worry about things a bit less, eh, love? Except for your maths.'

Oliver wanted to tell Mum he hadn't imagined it. Before he could, one of the people in Mum's office came out and tugged the sleeve of Mum's jacket and put a phone into her hand. Mum tried to push the phone away, but the person whispered to her, and Oliver could see it was urgent.

'Sorry, love,' Mum said to Oliver. 'We'll have to talk later at home. Hayden will look after you now.'

She gave Oliver a kiss on the cheek, went back into her office and closed the door.

After a moment she opened it again.

'How many?' she said.

'Seven out of twenty,' said Oliver.

Mum sighed and gave him a sympathetic look. She started to say something, but one of the people in her office tapped her on the shoulder and pointed to the phone in her hand. Mum wearily closed the door again.

Hayden came over.

'Come on, mate,' he said. 'The lift's this way.'

Oliver started to thank Hayden and remind him that people in year five could find their own way to lifts. But Hayden was already striding ahead.

Oliver decided to do some walking and talking.

'Hayden,' he said, catching up. 'When an investment turns into poo, will the bank ever give the person their money back if they really need it?'

Hayden stared at him, then chuckled all the way to the lift.

Oliver assumed that meant no.

It didn't seem fair.

'Why not?' said Oliver. 'The bank can afford to give them some money back. You've got millions.'

'That's right, we have,' said Hayden. 'And that's the whole point. We're big. We can't worry about every little investor. It's like when you build a sandcastle. Sometimes grains of sand roll off the sides. But if you want a big castle, you don't stop and worry about every little grain.'

Oliver thought about this.

Before he could explain the difference to Hayden between people and grains of sand, the lift doors opened.

'You're a very lucky boy,' said Hayden. 'Your parents are building a very big sandcastle. One day you're going to be a very rich man.'

In the lift, while Oliver watched the numbers flicker from eighteen all the way down to one, he tried to tell himself that Hayden was an idiot who didn't know what he was talking about.

Trouble was, Hayden had a PhD in Applied Mathematics, Mum had said.

Which means, thought Oliver sadly, Hayden probably does know what he's talking about.

The bank isn't going to give Nancy her money back, and unless I can get it for her, an innocent dog will die.

# 4

Oliver was feeling too anxious to stay in his bedroom, so he went out onto his balcony and stood staring at the lights of the city.

At night there were squillions.

Normally he found them relaxing to look at, specially the ones on the eighteenth floor of Mum and Dad's bank building across town. If he used his binoculars, he could see their office windows. Some evenings he was sure he could actually see them, working late into the night and getting even richer.

Tonight he didn't even bother looking.

All he could think about was a poor scared dog. Barclay was out there somewhere, probably locked in the ute and terrified.

Oliver spent a few minutes trying to spot the ute with his binoculars. But he couldn't see all the city streets, not even from up here in the penthouse, not even if he squinted till his eyeballs hurt.

'Don't worry, Barclay,' whispered Oliver. 'I'll get the money somehow.'

He looked at the list he'd made on his iPad of the things he could sell. Starting with his iPad. Followed by his computer, his Xbox, his PlayStation, his 3D-TV, his blu-ray burner, his leather jacket, his binoculars, his noise-suppression headphones, his skis (never used) and his souvenir test footy bedside lamp (only used with a forty-watt bulb).

Three thousand dollars for the lot if he was lucky. Buyers could be really stingy on eBay, Oliver had checked.

Plus nine hundred and eleven dollars in his savings account.

Grand total, three thousand nine hundred and eleven dollars.

It wasn't enough.

Numbers didn't lie, not when you used a calculator.

Oliver stared at the moon floating in the dark sky like a big zero.

Seven thousand and eighty-nine dollars more. That's what he needed to save Barclay's life. And he didn't have a clue how he was going to get it.

Oliver sat at the dining table eating his dinner and wondering if there was anything else in the apartment he could sell that Mum and Dad wouldn't notice missing.

Small things would be best. Dad's spare diamond

cufflinks. Or Mum's expensive Italian shoes, just the ones she didn't wear any more. Or the very small genuine eighteenth-century antique painting in the guest toilet. Or the remote for the car, which Dad was always moaning cost heaps to replace each time a driver lost it.

'Oliver, what's wrong?'

Oliver looked up, startled.

Vickey had come out from the kitchen.

For a second he was tempted to tell her everything. But he didn't. Vickey was very strict about not doing more than she was paid for, and Oliver was pretty sure she wasn't paid to save dogs from killer ex-housekeepers.

'You're not eating,' said Vickey. 'Don't you like it?'

Her face was pink from cooking and her curly hair was drooping from the steam. Oliver felt sorry for her because he knew how cross Mum got with housekeepers if he didn't eat properly.

'It's delicious,' said Oliver, taking a mouthful of lobster wrapped in bacon.

'So eat it,' said Vickey. 'I knock off soon.'

'You're a really good cook,' said Oliver. 'You should go on telly.'

Vickey rolled her eyes.

'I mean it,' said Oliver.

He did. If Vickey got sacked, at least after being on telly she could open her own restaurant or invent a chopping board.

'If I went on telly,' said Vickey, 'I wouldn't want

to cook, no way. I'd do something that didn't make my hair go flat. Like hosting a glamorous lifestyle show about rich people. I could start with you lot. I heard your dad say this dining table cost twenty-eight thousand dollars.'

Oliver stared at the table.

'I know,' said Vickey, going back into the kitchen. 'Ridiculous, eh?'

But Oliver only half-heard her because he was deep in thought.

Oliver lay in bed, too excited to sleep.

He'd been through the plan umpteen times in his head and he was pretty sure it would work.

There were three simple stages.

(1) Use his savings to buy a table that looked like the real dining table (yellowy-coloured wood with specks in it) but was much cheaper.

(2) Advertise the real dining table on eBay.

(3) Sell it for eleven thousand dollars.

(4) Give Nancy her money and save Barclay's life.

OK, four stages, but it couldn't fail.

Could it?

All around Oliver's room, tiny red and green and orange lights glowed and winked in the darkness.

'Too risky,' they seemed to be saying.

Oliver sighed.

They were smart, his Xbox and PlayStation and

iPad and blu-ray burner and 3D-TV and noise-suppression headphones, but sometimes they worried too much.

'Mum and Dad'll never notice,' said Oliver. 'They only eat at that table about once a year.'

He realised he was doing it again.

This is pathetic, he thought. I'm talking to electrical goods like they're pets.

Oliver rolled over in bed so he wouldn't have to look at the winking lights. As he did, he heard Mum and Dad come out of the lift into the living room.

A few moments later, Mum crept in.

'Are you still awake?' she whispered.

She sat on Oliver's bed and switched on his bedside lamp.

'I've been thinking about your visit to the bank this afternoon,' she said. 'You looked so stressed.'

Oliver opened his eyes. Mum reached out and held his shoulders tight. She looked at him with a strange expression. Sort of sad.

Suddenly he wanted to tell her about Nancy and Barclay again. So at least she'd understand later on if she spotted the dining table was missing.

'Mum . . .' he said.

She put her finger over his lips.

'Shhh,' she said. 'I need to say this. Me and Dad know we work very long hours. We wish we could be at home more. But we're doing it all for you, love. For your future. So you'll be safe and secure. You do know that, don't you?'

'Yes,' said Oliver.

He tried to give her a grateful smile.

'We owe you a lot of time, love,' said Mum. 'One day we'll pay you back. In a couple of years we'll be able to sell the bank and retire, and then we can be together as a family. Which'll be wonderful.'

Oliver nodded.

It would be. Really wonderful.

'Go to sleep now,' said Mum, kissing him on the head and switching off the lamp. 'Sweet dreams.'

Oliver opened his mouth to have one more try at telling her about Barclay, but she'd gone.

'Night,' he said sadly.

He closed his eyes and thought about how you can't tell somebody something if they don't want to hear it. He'd learned that from the electrical goods.

A couple of moments later, Dad came in and sat on the bed and switched the lamp back on.

'G'day mate,' he whispered. 'You still awake?'

Oliver opened his eyes and nodded.

He decided not to try to tell Dad about Nancy and Barclay. Dad would probably listen, but Oliver had a horrible vision of the army being rung and of an entire ute, including a small dog, being torn apart by SAS gunfire.

'I just want to put your mind at rest,' said Dad. 'About any rumours you might have heard.'

Oliver looked at him.

'Rumours?' he said.

'There's been some stuff in the news lately,' said Dad. 'About investment banks like ours having problems. It's all just gossip. Our bank's fine, so you don't have to worry.'

Oliver tried not to.

He also tried not to think about Barclay.

It wasn't easy.

'Anyway,' said Dad, 'even if things do get a bit wobbly out there for a while, we'll be OK. Our bank's been successful for a long time. We're too big to fail.'

Dad looked happy at this thought. Oliver wasn't so sure. He remembered hearing at school how Freddie MacLaren's big brother, who was the tallest kid in his high school, had run into a goalpost and got concussion and flunked year twelve. So you were never too big to fail.

Oliver decided not to bring that up now. He had something more important to talk about.

'Dad,' he said quietly. 'When an investment turns into poo, why can't you give the person their money back if they really need it?'

Dad sighed.

'That's what I'm talking about, son,' he said. 'If we start giving money back, word will get out. Gossip and rumours will start. Look what they're doing, people will say. Something dodgy must be going on at that bank.'

'Being kind isn't dodgy,' said Oliver.

Dad took a deep breath.

'In the banking business,' he said, 'rumours are like tumours. Once they start they're very hard to stop. You have to trust me, Ollie, and not worry your head about it. This is complicated stuff. You need a PhD in maths to really understand it.'

Oliver closed his eyes and wondered if there was a brain operation that would turn you into a maths genius. It must be possible. Medical science could do incredible things if you had the money.

Maybe he could get one for his birthday instead of a hang-glider.

'In a couple of years,' said Dad, 'things are going to be very different for this family. It'll be great. We'll be ready to move the bank to New York. Up there with the big boys.'

Oliver didn't say anything.

Mum must have forgotten about that plan.

'Exciting, eh?' said Dad. 'Sweet dreams, son.'

'Night,' said Oliver as Dad went out.

Dad was wrong. Oliver wasn't feeling even a tiny bit excited. And he knew he wouldn't be having sweet dreams.

Later, after Mum and Dad had gone to bed, Oliver gave up trying to go to sleep. He crept out into the living room, opened the blinds and stood in the moonlight, staring at the dining table.

Maybe things would be different in New York.

Maybe a New York school would be better at teaching maths and he'd learn lots of it.

And then he'd be able to talk about it with Mum and Dad, while they had breakfast and dinner with him every day.

At this table.

Oliver ran his hand over the smooth wood glowing gold in the moonlight.

Did he really want to be a burglar in his own home? The son of two brilliant high-finance maths geniuses, and all he could do was steal from his own parents?

No, he didn't.

But how else could he get Nancy's money?

If only he had relatives who could help. Other ones, not Granny and Grandpop, who lived on a cruise boat and never called, or Uncle Roy who was a monk in New Zealand, or Dad's parents who were killed in a train crash when Dad was two.

Oliver sighed.

His body sagged with tiredness.

Then, as he turned to go back to bed, something caught his eye.

On the grand piano (never used) was a silver picture frame.

Oliver went over and picked it up.

It was worth a few hundred dollars, but that wasn't what interested him.

In the frame was a photo of Dad at university, grinning, both thumbs up, a man with a big future.

Except back then, Oliver thought, Dad didn't look much like a maths genius.

He looked like a bit of a nerd.

Suddenly Oliver felt a stab of excitement as he stared at the photo.

Maybe Dad started making big bikkies before he got to be a maths genius. Maybe Mum did too. Maybe making big bikkies was something that some people could just naturally do.

If Dad did it, thought Oliver, and if Mum did . . . I'm their son.

Maybe I can too.

# 5

'What do you mean, buy shares in you?' said Freddie MacLaren, staring at Oliver doubtfully.

Oliver led Freddie to a quieter part of the playground, away from the other boys. He didn't want anyone else hearing about his idea just yet. Not till he had a chance to test it out on someone who wouldn't mock. Who he hoped was Freddie, based on the sympathetic looks Freddie sometimes gave him in class when the results of maths tests were read out.

'Shares,' said Oliver. 'It's when you buy part of a company or business, and instead of taking your part home, you let them still use it, and to say thank you they give you some of their profits.'

He was pretty sure that was right.

'I know what shares are,' said Freddie. 'My dad owns three per cent of Pizza Hut. But you're not Pizza Hut. You're not even a business. How can you sell shares in yourself?'

Oliver took a deep breath. Dad reckoned you could make anybody invest in anything if you explained it to them properly.

'When I leave school,' said Oliver, 'I'm going to have a pet shop. A really successful one with happy animals and room for browsing. I'm going to work really hard and make lots of money. Each year I'll give some of the money to the people who own a share in me.'

Oliver hoped he'd said it right. Mum and Dad talked about this stuff a lot, but Oliver didn't always catch the details. Often he was in bed, or watching them through binoculars.

'Why are you doing this?' said Freddie. 'Have your parents stopped your pocket money?'

Oliver decided to risk telling Freddie. It might encourage him to be sympathetic and buy the first share.

'I need eleven thousand dollars by next week,' said Oliver.

Freddie looked stunned.

'Why?' he asked.

'It's personal,' said Oliver.

'What's personal?' said a loud voice.

Oliver turned. And sagged. Standing there were three boys he was pretty sure wouldn't be sympathetic. Nathan Fisher, Cam Paulson and Lachlan Bernanke.

'Newton's selling shares in himself,' said Freddie.

Oliver tried to look relaxed.

The three boys stared at Oliver, then fell about laughing.

Oliver waited for them to finish so he could explain. But as soon as they stopped laughing, they started jeering.

'An investment in no-hoper Newton,' said Nathan Fisher. 'That'd be worth about four cents.'

Oliver could feel his face getting hot. He reminded himself that insults weren't as bad as what Barclay was facing.

'Two cents a share,' said Cam Paulson. 'That's my final offer.'

Oliver looked at the boys with what he hoped was the quiet dignity of an investment banker.

'They're fifty dollars each,' he said.

The boys howled even louder than before.

Freddie MacLaren joined in.

Oliver wondered if he'd set his Initial Public Offer price a bit too high. Fifty dollars had felt right. Google reckoned it was the average weekly year-five pocket money in Australian boys schools with very high fees.

Maybe I should have deducted an amount for lollies, thought Oliver.

The laughter was slowly dying down. Oliver hoped the boys were starting to see the Blue Sky Upside Benefits of the proposed investment.

They weren't.

'Here's your problem, dumbo,' said Lachlan Bernanke, poking Oliver in the chest. 'You're a dumbo. Your parents have spent thousands on maths tutors and you're still bottom of the class. Who'd want a part of you?'

Oliver didn't reply. He knew if he tried to, his voice would go wobbly. Because nobody had ever tried harder at maths than him. Not Mum, not Dad, not Bill Gates, not that kid on TV who could do really big sums in his head.

The boys were wandering off.

'The only investment I'd be interested in,' said Nathan Fisher to the other boys, 'is if I could double my money by lunchtime.'

The other boys laughed.

'OK,' called Oliver. 'You're on.'

The boys slowed down.

'I mean it,' said Oliver.

The boys turned and looked at Oliver. They walked slowly back to him.

'Invest fifty dollars in me now,' said Oliver, 'and I'll give you a hundred at lunchtime.'

The boys looked at each other.

Oliver hoped Dad was right when he said that sometimes you had to lose money to make money. And that deep down, everybody was greedy.

Nathan was looking uncertain.

'Newton's parents are investment bankers,' said Freddie MacLaren. 'Maybe he knows how to do this stuff.'

'Call his bluff, Nate,' said Lachlan Bernanke. 'If he doesn't pay up, we'll help you do him.'

'OK,' said Nathan to Oliver. 'A hundred at lunchtime. And if you don't pay up, you have to give me your phone.'

Oliver nodded.

Nathan hesitated for a moment, then pulled out his wallet.

At lunchtime, Oliver gave Nathan a hundred dollars.

Nathan looked a bit stunned.

So did Lachlan and Cam and Freddie, who'd been getting ready to do some debt collecting of the physical kind.

'Nice to do business with you,' said Oliver to Nathan.

He turned away with what he hoped was the confident expression of a successful investment banker.

'Hang on,' said Nathan. 'Can I invest some more?'

Oliver turned back.

'Alright,' he said to Nathan. 'Same deal. Pay fifty now, you get a hundred tomorrow morning.'

Nathan nodded eagerly.

'I'll have one too,' said Lachlan.

'And me,' said Cam.

'And me,' said Freddie.

Oliver pulled some investment certificates from his blazer pocket. They were actually used detention forms he'd found in the school recycling bin, but he'd crossed out all the detention stuff and written the investment stuff next to it.

The boys handed him fifty-dollar notes.

Oliver gave them an investment certificate each. He tried not to show them how excited he was.

His plan was working.

That evening Oliver had a look at his assets and liabilities. He spread them out on his bed.

He had one thousand and sixty-one dollars in cash, which included all the money from his savings account, plus the fifty-dollar notes he'd got from Nathan, Lachlan, Cam and Freddie, minus the hundred dollars he'd paid to Nathan.

He was pretty sure that added up to one thousand and sixty-one dollars, because he'd done the sums on the calculator three times and counted the cash eleven times.

So, said Oliver to himself, that's my assets.

He knew they were called assets because Mum and Dad were always using the word to describe things they had, like buildings and housekeepers.

Oliver picked up his iPad and looked at the list he'd made of his liabilities.

*Nathan Fisher $100*
*Cam Paulson $100*
*Lachlan Bernanke $100*
*Freddie MacLaren $100*

Oliver knew the money you had to pay out was called liabilities because he'd heard Mum use the expression when housekeepers got parking tickets.

This is good, thought Oliver. My assets are more than my liabilities.

He'd checked, and Google reckoned that when your assets were more than your liabilities, your business was in a healthy state. Which, Google also said, was the way to attract more investors.

Excellent.

Oliver sometimes wondered how kids whose parents worked sixteen-hour days got information before Google was invented.

He heard Vickey calling him for dinner.

Before he went to the dining table, Oliver popped out onto his balcony and held his thumbs up. He knew Barclay probably couldn't see him, but dogs had a sixth sense and he wanted Barclay to know that things were going really well.

# 6

Next morning things started going wrong.

Oliver knew he had a problem as soon as he reached the playground and saw the crowd of boys running towards him waving fifty-dollar notes.

Word had obviously spread to year six as well. The excited crowd clamouring around him was huge. Which was good, in a way.

Oliver's calculator had told him that to pay Nancy her eleven thousand dollars he needed to sell two hundred and twenty shares at fifty dollars each.

What wasn't so good were the things the crowd was yelling at him.

'Double it.'

'Double my money.'

'Double mine too.'

Oliver glanced over his shoulder to make sure Vickey had driven off. He looked around the playground to make sure all the teachers were either in the staffroom having coffee or in the car park comparing cars.

Then he held up his hands for silence.

Which, to his amazement, he got. The crowd gazed at him, waiting for him to speak. Oliver started to understand why investment bankers on TV always looked so full of themselves.

'Yesterday,' he said to the crowd, 'was a special offer.'

He hoped that was the right expression. Google had been a bit vague on the subject of doubling money by lunchtime.

'From today,' continued Oliver, 'shares in me will still double your money, but you won't get it for a while.'

Oliver looked around nervously at the crowd. He hoped they wouldn't mind that last bit. They shouldn't if they were genuine long-term investors, which Dad always said were the best kind.

The crowd was scowling and glaring at him.

They did seem to mind.

'Oliver Newton shares are an investment for the future,' explained Oliver. 'You buy them now and they pay you lots in the future. That's why they're called futures.'

He hoped that was right. He'd heard Mum and Dad use the word, but maybe they were just talking about future housekeepers.

'Cheat,' somebody yelled. 'You said you'd double our money today.'

Oliver tried to explain he'd only promised that to four shareholders. The crowd didn't seem to understand. Everybody started yelling and demanding to have their money doubled right now.

Luckily the bell went.

But the crowd didn't go. They rushed at Oliver, trying to stuff fifty-dollar notes into his hands and pockets.

Oliver was jostled and pummelled to the ground. He peered anxiously through the scrum of legs. Any minute now, teachers would round everyone up for assembly. And selling shares in the playground was almost certainly against school rules.

Boldly and decisively, Oliver did what he was pretty sure any investment banker would do to break up a crowd and not get into trouble with teachers.

He took all the money and agreed to double it by tomorrow.

That night Oliver lay in bed, staring at his iPad, worrying about his assets and liabilities.

His assets were quite a lot.

He had six hundred and sixty-one dollars of yesterday's assets left after paying Nathan, Cam, Lachlan and Freddie their one hundred dollars each. He also had two thousand three hundred dollars of new assets, which is what all the fifty-dollar investments added up to after he'd pulled them out of his pockets and school bag and socks.

Total assets, two thousand nine hundred and sixty-one dollars.

Not enough to save Barclay's life, but not bad for a start.

What was worrying Oliver were his liabilities. At lunchtime tomorrow in the playground, forty-six investors were expecting to get double their money back. And some of them did karate.

Total liabilities, four thousand six hundred dollars.

And possibly a few broken bones.

Oliver tried to imagine what Mum and Dad would do in this situation.

Dad was always saying the secret of successful investment banking was trust. You couldn't make big bikkies if your clients didn't trust you.

What I need, thought Oliver, is a way of making the other kids trust me. So they won't mind if I don't pay them back just yet.

'Mr Langrish, sir, can I ask you something, please?'

Oliver hurried across the staff car park to where Mr Langrish was climbing out of his old sports car.

'What is it?' said Mr Langrish suspiciously.

Oliver knew why his class teacher wasn't pleased to see him. The last time Oliver had asked Mr Langrish a question before school, it hadn't worked out well. Mr Langrish had explained long division to Oliver yet again, but Oliver still hadn't understood and Mr Langrish had missed his morning coffee.

'It's not about long division,' said Oliver.

'Good,' said Mr Langrish.

'It's about the maths project,' said Oliver. 'You know, sir, the one where we have to choose an example of maths in society and write four hundred words about it.'

'Yes,' said Mr Langrish. 'I do know. I set it.'

'Well,' said Oliver, 'I've finished mine.'

'Really,' said Mr Langrish, not looking very impressed. 'That's probably just as well as it was due in yesterday.'

He looked even less impressed when Oliver handed him a slightly crumpled sheet of paper.

Mr Langrish glanced at his watch.

'It's about credit default swaps, sir,' said Oliver. 'Credit default swaps are a type of insurance that investors buy in case their investments go bung. Going bung means not getting your money back. With insurance you do get it back.'

Oliver paused for breath.

Mr Langrish looked at Oliver, then at the project, then at Oliver again.

'Did your parents do this for you?' he asked.

Oliver was shocked that Mr Langrish would even think such a thing.

'No, sir,' he said. 'I did it all myself. And I changed the Google sentences around like you told us to.'

'Very good,' said Mr Langrish, glancing at his watch again.

'Can you mark it now, please, sir?' said Oliver.

'No,' said Mr Langrish. 'I haven't had my coffee yet. You'll get it back in class with everyone else.'

As Mr Langrish walked away, Oliver remembered the other thing he'd meant to say.

'Please, sir,' he called. 'I need a good mark. By lunchtime.'

Just before the lunch bell went, Oliver's insides gave a little leap. Mr Langrish was putting down his marking pen and picking up the bundle of projects from his desk.

'Paulson,' he said. 'Footy scores. Not the most riveting example of maths in society, but not bad. Bernanke, kill totals in Warcraft, predictable. Ling, lolly prices, your work's improving. Newton, credit default swaps . . .'

Mr Langrish paused at Oliver's desk.

Oliver had trouble breathing.

'. . . unexpected,' said Mr Langrish. 'And, I have to say, impressive.'

He dropped the sheet of paper onto Oliver's desk and moved on.

Oliver grabbed it and gazed happily at the red squiggle in the corner.

The lunchtime investors meeting was rowdy, with a lot of angry shouting.

Oliver was glad he'd decided to hold it on the other side of the footy oval, well away from any teachers.

First he asked if anyone had any questions.

Lots of people did.

The same question.

'Where's our money?'

Oliver waited for the shouting to die down. Then, before any karate could begin, he told the meeting how sometimes investments could be a bit late paying up. But, he quickly added, there was no need for stress because insurance was available to guarantee that everyone would get their money.

He held up a bundle of credit-default-swap certificates, which he'd been up half the night making out of pages torn from his maths exercise book.

'Only five dollars each,' he said.

The meeting was still a bit doubtful and suspicious.

Oliver reminded them that his parents ran an investment bank, so he knew about this stuff. Then he showed them how Mr Langrish had given credit default swaps an A+.

Suddenly the meeting was rowdy again, but only because everybody wanted one.

After school, Oliver took refuge in the toilets and locked himself in a cubicle with his school bag.

He needed the school bag to carry all the cash.

Once he'd explained how credit default swaps meant nobody would lose anything, there'd been a blizzard of money that hadn't stopped, mostly from new shares. That's why Oliver needed time in the toilets, so he could take a breather and count today's assets.

Oliver counted them. He counted them again. It was incredible, so he counted them a third time.

Seven thousand eight hundred and twenty-five dollars.

He tapped the numbers into the calculator. He added the amount he had at home.

Grand total, ten thousand seven hundred and eighty-six dollars.

Only two hundred and fourteen dollars to go and then he could pay Nancy back. And it was only Thursday afternoon and he had till Monday to do it.

Barclay was saved.

Oliver would have shouted with joy, except shouting in the toilets was against school rules.

Plus, underneath the joy, Oliver was feeling a bit anxious.

It was to do with his liabilities. Sooner or later he'd have to give everyone double their money back. About twenty thousand dollars, as far as he could work out.

The only way he could get twenty thousand dollars was to sell another *tap*, *tap*, four hundred share certificates.

But then he'd have to pay, *tap*, *tap*, forty thousand dollars back.

If he sold forty thousand dollars' worth of shares, he'd have to pay eighty thousand dollars back.

And so on.

*Tap, tap, tap.*

Oliver stared at the cash in his school bag.

Cash he didn't have two days ago.

Thanks to the miracle of investment banking, money could be made out of nothing. You could get rich. A dog's life could be saved. It was a brilliant system, more brilliant than Oliver had ever dreamed when he started it. But there was one little thing he hadn't thought of until now.

'Help,' whispered Oliver, alone in the cubicle. 'I don't know how to stop.'

# 7

Oliver told the security man in the foyer of Mum and Dad's bank building that he was here to see Hayden Dorevitch.

Just Hayden.

Mum's assistant.

Nobody else.

'I get the picture,' said the security man, picking up his phone.

Oliver doubted that he did. The picture was looking very grim. Oliver had worked out that if he kept selling new investments to pay back the old ones, in a couple of weeks he'd owe the kids at school more than eighty million dollars.

He was pretty sure even the most successful pet shop in the world couldn't earn that much.

Oliver waited impatiently by the lift doors, desperately hoping there was something Hayden could tell him that would explain where he'd gone wrong. Something he'd missed in year five maths.

Otherwise he'd have to find another way to save Barclay. And there were only three days left.

'Hi, Ollie, what's happening?'

Hayden came out of the lift.

Oliver kept his voice low so they wouldn't be overheard.

'I need your help,' he said.

'Walk and talk,' said Hayden, steering him into the lift. 'Things are going crazy upstairs.'

By the time Oliver explained the problem to Hayden in a way that made it sound like a maths project, and managed to do it without mentioning Nancy or Barclay, and told Hayden not to bother Mum and Dad with any of it, the lift had reached the eighteenth floor.

'The thing I don't get about investment banking,' said Oliver, 'is how to stop.'

Hayden gave him a grin.

'That's the whole point,' said Hayden as they stepped out of the lift. 'We never have to.'

Oliver stared at him.

Was he joking?

No, he wasn't.

'Keep the money moving,' said Hayden. 'That's the secret. Never stop and the big bikkies keep rolling in. You can put that in your homework if you like.'

'But what if you owe so much,' said Oliver, 'you can't ever pay it back?'

Hayden thought about this.

'That's when you have to be too big to fail,' he said.

Oliver frowned. Dad had said that too.

'What does too big to fail mean?' asked Oliver.

'Simple,' said Hayden. 'Why don't big banks ever go broke? Because we're too important. If we get in the poo, the government gets us out. Pays our debts. Good, eh? But don't put that in your homework. Not many people know that. It's our little secret, right?'

Oliver nodded doubtfully.

It was an interesting secret, but it didn't help much. Oliver was pretty sure he knew what the government would say if he asked them to give eighty million dollars to the kids at school.

'Got to go,' said Hayden. 'The share market's a dead cat today.'

Oliver wished Hayden wouldn't use financial expressions involving pets.

'Bye,' he said to Hayden. 'Thanks.'

Hayden hurried into the trading room.

Oliver saw what was happening in there. People were running around waving phones and pointing at screens and yelling at each other. Dad included.

They looked even more stressed than usual.

Oliver envied them. They were lucky. They were big. They had millions of dollars to play with, and millions more from the government any time they needed it.

He sighed.

It was all very well being too big to fail, but what could you do when you were too small to succeed? And a dog was depending on you?

Oliver was about to turn away when he saw something on the other side of the trading room. In Mum's office, behind the frosted glass, was the silhouette of somebody sitting with their head in their hands.

They looked upset.

Oliver hurried over, just about managing not to get trampled by frantic maths geniuses.

He tapped on Mum's door.

No reply.

He opened it and peeked in. Mum was slumped in her office chair, staring out the window.

'I said no interruptions,' she snapped.

Then she looked up and saw it was him.

'Sorry, love,' she said. 'I thought you were Hayden. What are you doing here? Where's Vickey?'

'Downstairs in the car,' said Oliver. 'Are you alright?'

Mum gave a long sigh.

'We're having a bit of a stressful day,' she said.

Oliver went over and gave her a hug. A cautious one. Usually she didn't like being hugged in the office. But today it was OK, she let him.

He made it a long one.

'Sometimes,' said Mum, almost to herself, 'I wish we didn't have this bank. I wish we had your pet shop instead.'

Oliver thought she was joking. But there was something in her voice that didn't sound like a joke, and when he looked at her more closely he saw she meant it.

He didn't know what to say. He'd never seen Mum looking so miserable. Not even the times she tried to ring Granny and Grandpop on the cruise ship and their phone was always turned off.

Oliver hugged her again.

I know why she's so sad, he thought. It's because she's got a kind heart and she can't bear seeing even a few investors in the poo.

'Mum,' said Oliver. 'I think I might know how to help.'

Mum looked at him.

'The customers who lost their money,' he said. 'Why don't you say you gave them a credit default swap each for their birthday last year and forgot to tell them? Which means now they're insured, and you're allowed to pay them the money they lost after all.'

Mum closed her eyes.

For a moment Oliver thought it was because she was so moved by the brilliance of the idea.

When she opened them again, he saw it wasn't.

'Thanks for trying, love,' she said gently. 'But you're in a bit over your head here. Why don't you go home with Vickey and I'll see you later.'

She kissed him on the cheek, stood up and steered him to the door.

Mum's right, thought Oliver as he waited for the lift. I am in over my head.

At school tomorrow he had to make a choice. Give up trying to make the money to save Barclay, or end up owing millions.

Oliver sighed.

He knew what he had to do and he wasn't looking forward to it.

# 8

'I don't want it back,' said Lachlan Bernanke, outraged. 'No way. Get lost.'

Oliver ignored him and stuffed fifty-seven dollars into Lachlan's pocket.

He'd known it would be difficult, giving all his investors their money back, but he hadn't realised it would be this difficult.

Lachlan pulled the fifty-seven dollars out and stuffed it into Oliver's pocket.

'I don't want it back till it's doubled,' said Lachlan. 'You can have more time, but I want it doubled.'

For a few weary seconds Oliver was tempted to keep the money. It would be the easy way to save Barclay. But then he thought of the eighty million dollars he'd owe in a couple of weeks. And how disappointed Mum and Dad would be with him when they had to pay it.

Oliver looked at the crowd of angry investors milling around him in the playground. He tried to think how Dad would deal with this problem.

He'd be honest, that's how.

'I'm sorry,' Oliver yelled to the crowd. 'I can't do this any more. I made a mistake. I got the maths wrong.'

'That'd be right,' said Nathan Fisher bitterly.

'Shut up,' said a year-six investor to Nathan. 'If you start a rumour he's rubbish at maths, there'll be widespread panic.'

'But he *is* rubbish at maths,' said Nathan.

The crowd started to look anxious. Muttering and jostling broke out.

Oliver held up his hands for silence.

He didn't get it.

'I'm trying to be fair,' he shouted. 'Nobody'll lose their money. Everyone'll get their fifty-dollar investment back, and their five-dollar credit-default-swap fee, plus two dollars interest. So each of you will get, um . . .'

His stressed brain wouldn't do the sum. He counted the money he was holding in his hand.

'Fifty-seven dollars,' said Oliver. 'The two dollars interest is from me to say thank you because I've had your money for a day or two. It's a fair amount, ask any investment banker.'

The crowd glared at him sullenly.

'If you don't agree,' said Oliver, 'I'll have to go bankrupt and place all the money in the hands of an administrator. That's what Google says would have to happen.'

The investors looked alarmed.

'The administrator would probably be Mr Langrish,' said Oliver.

'You can't do that,' said Jai Fleming. 'Mr Langrish wouldn't give us a cent till we'd handed in all this term's maths projects.'

The investors looked even more worried.

Oliver held out the fifty-seven dollars to Lachlan Bernanke.

Sulkily, Lachlan took it.

The other investors grumpily stuck out their hands too. Oliver unzipped his school bag. As he gave back fistfuls of cash, he could see from everyone's faces that they'd never forgive him. Life at school would be even more miserable from now on.

Oliver tried not to think about that.

He had something bigger to worry about. It was Friday afternoon. In two days Barclay would be facing the knife.

Oliver glanced at his phone to see if Nancy had replied to his text. The one he'd sent earlier that morning, begging her for more time and promising to come up with a new idea to get her the money very soon.

Nothing.

'Do you know what you are?' said Lachlan Bernanke, putting his face close to Oliver's. 'You're a no-hoper. You want to be a big shot, but you haven't got what it takes. Say hello to your loser life, dumbo.'

The other investors jeered their agreement.

Oliver struggled not to get angry and start a fight. He pretended to be busy with something in his bag.

As he did, a voice yelled out across the playground.

'Which of you mongrels is Oliver Newton?'

All the investors hesitated.

Then pointed at Oliver.

Oliver's insides froze. For a second he thought it was Nancy, coming for him, knife in hand.

But it wasn't.

It was a girl, walking angrily towards him. She was about his age with a mass of tangled yellow hair and torn jeans and a faded t-shirt and a furious face.

She stopped in front of Oliver, glaring at him. She was a bit taller than him, which made Oliver feel even more nervous.

'Oliver Newton?' she said.

Oliver could see she was extremely angry.

He hesitated.

The investors, who'd been a bit stunned at the sight of a girl in the school grounds, all nodded.

The girl punched Oliver in the tummy, hard.

Oliver doubled over, choking with pain, and sank to the ground.

'That's for your parents killing my dad,' said the girl.

Oliver lay curled up in agony, eyes closed, trying to make sense of what she'd just said.

Mum and Dad?

Kill someone?

Impossible.

Oliver was desperate to ask the girl what she meant, but he couldn't speak. When he finally managed to take a painful breath and open his eyes, she'd gone. All he could see were investors, staring down at him, stunned.

'Oh poop,' muttered Lachlan Bernanke, looking at him nervously. 'I've just insulted someone whose parents are in the mafia.'

'One other thing,' came the girl's voice.

Oliver rolled over. The girl was almost at the school gate, glaring back at him.

'You can forget about the dog,' she said.

She turned and walked out the gate.

Oliver stood up, trying to grab onto his scrambled thoughts.

Dog?

Was she talking about Barclay?

Oliver realised Nancy must have sent her.

He felt sick.

The bell went. The investors hurried into school. All except for Freddie MacLaren, who stayed behind, hovering.

'Your life's a total mess,' said Freddie to Oliver. 'Do you think you should talk to Ms Hinchley?'

Oliver shook his head. Ms Hinchley was the school counsellor. There'd be time for that later. Right now he had to find out what the girl had meant about Barclay. And about Mum and Dad.

'Thanks,' Oliver said to Freddie. 'I'll be fine.'

Freddie shrugged and went into school.

Oliver picked up his bag and hurried to the gate. He peered up and down the street.

There was the girl in the distance, standing in the bus shelter with her back to him.

Oliver took a few steps towards her, then stopped.

Talking to her probably wasn't the best idea. It would probably be him talking and her punching. If he wanted to find out what was happening to Barclay, the best idea was probably to follow her.

# 9

'So we're just gunna sit here, are we?' said the taxi driver.

Oliver peered through the windscreen past the school gate, to where the girl who'd punched him was getting on a bus.

'Just till that bus goes,' said Oliver, pointing. 'Then I'd like to follow it, please. But not too close.'

The driver gave Oliver a look, and started the engine.

'S'pose I should be grateful,' muttered the driver. 'If you weren't such a rich poshy, you'd be getting the bus yourself.'

Oliver didn't reply.

He scrabbled around in the bottom of his school bag, hoping there was a bit of money there that he hadn't given back to his investors.

Each time the bus stopped and the girl didn't get off, he groped for a bit more. By the time the bus stopped for about the tenth time, Oliver had found all the money that was left.

He watched the bus door anxiously. The girl still didn't get off. Oliver glanced at the taxi meter.

Thirty-eight dollars.

He counted his money.

Forty-six dollars.

That meant he only had . . . not much more. He hoped the girl got off soon.

Then he had another thought. If Nancy was a farmer now, this could be a very long ride.

Did city buses go to farms?

'Surprised a bloke like you has to count his cash,' said the taxi driver. 'Thought you'd be rolling in it.'

Oliver was tempted to say that an hour ago he'd had ten thousand seven hundred and eighty-one dollars. But he didn't.

The bus moved off again.

The taxi moved off too.

Oliver was finding it hard to concentrate on conversation. All he could think about was Barclay.

A hearse drove past in the opposite direction.

Do murdered pets get funerals? wondered Oliver sadly. Even if they don't have loving owners?

'Anyway,' said the taxi driver. 'What do they teach you at that poshy school? What have you learned this week?'

'A lot,' said Oliver quietly. 'For example, I've learned you can't use asset-backed derivatives to save a dog's life.'

The taxi driver didn't say anything after that.

Oliver stared out at the traffic as the taxi drove along behind the bus.

This is a bit like investment banking, thought Oliver. Everything's fine as long as we keep moving. The bad part doesn't happen till we stop.

The bus stopped again.

Forty-three dollars and sixty cents.

The girl got off.

'I'll get out here, thanks,' said Oliver, relieved.

While the taxi driver counted the money, Oliver could hear what sounded like a doggy tail eagerly thumping.

He realised it was his heart, thumping with hope that Barclay might still be alive despite everything.

Stay, Oliver said to himself.

What he desperately wanted to do was leap out of the taxi and sprint after the girl and follow her to Nancy and rescue Barclay. But he knew he had a better chance of doing that if he stayed out of sight for a bit.

Oliver got out of the taxi, crouched behind a telegraph pole and started counting to a hundred.

He switched on his phone map. When a dog was in danger, it was best to know where you were in case you had to call an ambulance.

As Oliver reached twenty-seven, two things happened. The taxi driver stopped staring at him and drove away, and the girl walked round a corner into a side street.

Oliver hurried along to the corner.

The girl clearly wasn't going to a farm. This wasn't even the countryside. It was a suburb with really small houses. There wasn't an office block to be seen. Or a penthouse. Most of the buildings didn't even have an upstairs.

Oliver paused at the corner. Peering round a hedge, he saw the girl go into one of the little houses halfway up the side street.

He counted to twenty-seven again, then crept cautiously towards the house.

Nancy's ute was parked in the driveway.

No sign of the girl, or Nancy.

The house was silent. Almost.

Oliver heard a moaning growling sound, like an animal in pain.

Oh no.

It was coming from the back of the house. Oliver hurried past the ute and along the side of the house, crouching so his head was below the windows. At the rear corner of the house he stopped, pressed himself against the wall and peeped round into the backyard.

There was Nancy by the washing line, holding the big knife.

Oliver looked around frantically for Barclay.

But the animal making the noise wasn't small and white with black splotches and a friendly tail and a quivering nose.

It was brown and huge, bigger than Nancy.

It had a big hump in the middle of its back.

Oliver stared.

A camel?

What was a camel doing in the backyard of a suburban house?

Oliver saw something else. The camel had a bandage on the side of its tummy. There were red patches on the bandage.

Blood.

Oliver felt ill.

Had Nancy stabbed the camel? Did a circus owe her money too?

Oliver took a deep breath and tried to calm down. That couldn't be right. If Nancy wanted to kill the camel, why was she feeding it? She was using the knife to carve chunks off a large biscuit, as big as a car wheel, and the camel was gobbling the chunks.

The camel turned and stared at Oliver.

Oliver gulped. The camel didn't look friendly. It gave a loud growl. Oliver, startled, took a hasty step back out of sight. And thudded into the wooden wall of the house.

'Who's there?' called Nancy. 'Is that you, Rose?'

Oliver squeezed himself against the house, hoping Nancy would think he was just the neighbour's water pipes being noisy.

But she didn't.

She appeared round the corner of the house, still holding the knife, glaring at him.

'Oliver?' she said. 'Oliver, what the –?'

Oliver kept his eyes on the knife. But only for a moment. Then a potato hit him in the head. He staggered back in pain and saw the raw potato spinning at his feet. It was peeled.

'You slimebag,' yelled a voice. 'I'll kill you, you mongrel.'

Another potato skimmed past his head, thudding into the side of the house.

Oliver ducked and peered desperately around, trying to work out how to get away from Killer Nancy. Then he saw it wasn't Nancy who was throwing the potatoes.

It was the girl with the yellow hair. She was holding a saucepan and a potato peeler.

'How dare you come here, you mongrel,' she shouted. 'We're in mourning, you slug.'

She threw the saucepan.

Oliver ducked again. The saucepan hit the wall above his head. Water and potatoes cascaded over him.

'Rose,' said Nancy. 'Stop it. You're upsetting Moo.'

Wiping the water out of his eyes, Oliver saw the camel was flinging its head around and twisting its body and trying to kick its legs out of the ropes that were loosely hobbling its feet.

Suddenly it succeeded and started running straight towards Oliver.

'Moo,' shouted Nancy. 'Hoosh.'

She grabbed at the rope hanging from the camel's head, but missed.

The camel swerved but didn't slow down. Oliver realised it was trying to get up the driveway to the street. He had a vision of the big graceful creature out in the traffic. Even a slow-moving car would make a mess of its long bony legs.

As the camel brushed past him, Oliver grabbed the rope. He was jerked flat onto the dusty driveway, and dragged painfully along it, but he hung on.

Finally the dragging stopped.

Oliver looked up.

The camel was gazing down at him with the biggest eyes Oliver had ever seen on an animal.

It looked annoyed.

Oliver heard Nancy yell something but he wasn't sure what.

Then one of the camel's legs moved in a blur and that was that.

# 10

'Oliver,' said a voice a long way away. 'Oliver.'

Oliver wondered where he was.

His head hurt, so he didn't open his eyes. His head hurt a lot. He wondered if he'd been attacked by disgruntled investors and bashed with a school bag full of two-dollar coins.

'Oliver.'

He recognised the voice.

It was Killer Nancy.

He tried to roll into a ball to protect himself.

'For pete's sake, Oliver,' said Nancy, sounding annoyed. 'Open your eyes. You got kicked in the head and I want to see if you're OK.'

Oliver opened his eyes.

And rolled himself even tighter. The camel was looming over him, eyes big and staring. Its big lips were moving over what Oliver was sure were huge teeth.

Then Oliver saw there was glass between him

and the camel. He was indoors and the camel was outside, looking at him through a window.

Oliver relaxed.

A bit.

He was lying on a scratchy old sofa that smelled. He was in a room about the size of Mum's walk-in wardrobe, except it was a living room.

Nancy was kneeling next to him, frowning and wiping his head with a damp towel. Over her shoulder, the girl was looking at him.

'He's not dead,' said the girl. 'Shame.'

'Rose,' said Nancy. 'Not now.'

Oliver winced as Nancy stuck a bandaid onto his forehead.

'You'll have to excuse Rose and Moo,' Nancy said. 'Rough time for them both. Moo got sick and needed an operation. We didn't have the money to fly a vet out to our farm, so we had to drag Moo to the city in that horse float out there.'

Oliver glanced nervously again at the camel. Behind it he could see the horse float, a tall narrow box on wheels, parked in the backyard.

Suddenly Oliver was almost blinded by a very bright light. Nancy was shining a torch into his eyes.

'OK,' she said. 'You haven't got concussion.'

As Oliver's eyes recovered, he remembered something with a jab of panic and sat up.

'Where's Barclay?' he said.

Oliver was still giddy and dazed, but he could tell that Nancy wasn't replying.

'Barclay the dog,' said Oliver. 'The one you took hostage.'

Nancy looked at him for a moment.

'He's not a hostage any more,' she said.

Oliver stared at her. He had a horrible vision of Barclay's poor stabbed body, buried somewhere in the garden.

'He's fine,' said Nancy. 'I gave him to my sister-in-law. She's out taking him for a walk.'

Oliver blinked, confused.

'You gave Barclay away?' he said.

'Not exactly gave,' said Nancy. 'I owe Gail money and she took the dog as part-payment.'

Oliver tried to see from Nancy's face if she was telling the truth. She looked a bit ashamed, but that was probably how a dog killer would look.

Nancy flipped open her phone.

'I'll call Gail,' she said. 'See when she'll be back.'

While Nancy made the call, Oliver tried to stay calm and not look at the girl, who was still glaring at him as if she was planning to attack him with more potatoes.

'If you'll be a while,' Nancy was saying into the phone, 'text me a photo of the dog. Got someone here who wants a squiz.'

Nancy closed the phone.

'Gail won't be back for a bit,' she said to Oliver. 'But when her text comes through, you'll see the dog's fine.'

Oliver was starting to feel relieved. And angry.

'You lied,' he said to Nancy. 'You made me think you were going to stab Barclay. I've been frantic. I've had tummy stress for days.'

Nancy didn't say anything.

But the girl did. She took a step towards Oliver.

'At least she's not a real killer,' said the girl. 'Not like your parents.'

Oliver glared back at her.

'What are you on about?' he said. 'They aren't –'

'Yes, they are,' shouted the girl. 'They murdered my father.'

Oliver stared at her. She was obviously mental. Her tangled yellow hair looked like a haystack on her head. Each strand looked as stiff as straw. It was probably stabbing her in the brain.

Nancy put her arms round the girl.

Slowly the girl stopped shaking.

'Rose,' said Nancy. 'Take Moo down to the other end of the yard. Auntie Gail won't want to find camel slobber on her windows when she gets back. You can give Moo another biscuit.'

'We've only got a few left,' muttered the girl.

She gave Oliver a long glare, then stamped out.

Oliver heard a thumping outside the window. He turned. The camel was nudging the windowpane with its lips, still staring at Oliver. But its eyes didn't look fierce any more. They looked sad. Big sad brown puddles.

The girl appeared, glared at Oliver through the glass, and led the camel down the backyard.

Oliver turned back to Nancy.

Before he could ask her what the girl was on about and inform her that Mum and Dad definitely hadn't killed anybody, Nancy's phone went ping.

Oliver jumped up.

The Barclay text.

Nancy opened her phone, looked at the screen, and her face went grim.

'Oh no,' she said.

'What?' said Oliver, alarmed.

He peered at the screen.

There was Barclay, alive and well, looking weary but hopeful. He was being held by a pudgy man wearing glasses and a death metal t-shirt.

'She promised,' Nancy muttered.

Nancy looked cross. And worried. Which was confusing, because Barclay looked fine.

'What's wrong?' said Oliver.

'That's Erik,' said Nancy. 'Gail's ex-husband.'

She hesitated.

Oliver could see there was something she didn't want to say.

'What?' he said.

'I told Gail the dog wasn't to go there,' said Nancy. 'Erik and his mates take dogs with them on their hunting trips in the bush. When they've had a few drinks, they can be . . . unkind to animals.'

Oliver stared at her.

'I'm going over there,' said Nancy. 'You wait here.'

She headed for the door. Oliver followed her. Nancy stopped and looked at him.

'OK,' she said, 'you come too. If they see you're upset, we might have a better chance of getting the dog back.'

## 11

Nancy drove fast down her street.

Oliver hung on in the front of the ute, trying not to worry about Barclay.

It was hard. The thought of Barclay on a hunting trip, being forced to drag huge dead kangaroos by cruel hunters, made Oliver's insides hurt.

And what if Barclay refused?

Nancy drove round the corner, past the bus stop and off in another direction.

Oliver switched on his phone map.

'I should never have trusted Gail with that dog,' muttered Nancy. 'Not when she's so angry with me about Tim.'

Oliver tried to work out what she meant.

'Who's Tim?' he said.

Nancy sighed.

'After your mother fired me,' she said, 'I went travelling and ended up with a bloke called Tim. Rose is his daughter. Her mum ran off to India when

Rose was a baby. Tim had a camel farm, outback treks with tourists and stuff. Everything was good for a few years, then the drought sent us broke.'

Nancy paused.

Oliver could see she was having painful memories.

'We borrowed money from Gail, Tim's sister. That soon went on camel feed and water. We tried to sell the camels. Gail said shoot them, but we couldn't. Our last resort was the money I'd invested. It was for Rose to go to uni one day. I called your parents' bank and discovered the money was in shares and something called collateralised debt somethings. Which are now worth dandruff.'

Oliver thought about this.

'Is that why Gail's done the bad thing with Barclay?' he asked. 'Because she's cross about the money you owe her?'

'Partly,' said Nancy, steering the ute into another street. 'Mostly it's because she blames me for what happened to Tim.'

Before Oliver could ask Nancy what that was, the ute pulled up in front of another small house.

Nancy jumped out. So did Oliver.

The front door was opened by a woman who was a bit older than Nancy, and taller.

'Thought you'd be over,' she said to Nancy.

She gave Oliver a brief glance.

'This the cops?' she said.

'You promised you wouldn't bring the dog here, Gail,' said Nancy. 'Where is it?'

'You're speaking to the wrong person,' said Gail. 'It's not my dog any more. Erik gave me four hundred bucks for it.'

Nancy pushed past her into the house. Oliver followed. They went into a small living room. Oliver peered around for Barclay. It was hard to see because the room was full of cigarette smoke and the curtains were closed and the ceiling was painted black.

Then Oliver heard an excited whimper.

'Barclay?' he said.

Barclay was being held tightly by pudgy Erik, who was sitting in a tattered armchair.

A couple of other men were sprawled around the room as well, grinning over cans of beer.

'We've come for the dog,' said Nancy.

The men chuckled.

'It was a mistake,' said Oliver. 'Nancy didn't know this was going to happen.'

Erik and the other men chuckled again.

'Have you got five hundred bucks?' Erik said to Oliver.

'Not at the moment,' said Oliver.

'Well then Barclay's gunna play with us for a while,' said Erik.

Oliver looked around for some way to get Barclay out of the room. And saw several shotguns leaning against the wall behind the TV.

Nancy was glaring at Gail.

Gail gave an angry laugh.

'Look at this,' Gail said to Oliver, pointing at Nancy. 'She's accusing me of not caring for the dog properly. Which is rich, coming from her. This is the woman who encouraged my brother Tim, a man who'd never drilled for water in his life, to borrow an old drill rig and haul it two hundred k's to their farm, just to try and get water for those stupid camels. And then she was shocked when the drill broke and bits flew off it and Tim was killed.'

Oliver stared at Gail and Nancy, taking this in.

'I didn't encourage him,' muttered Nancy. 'We were desperate.'

Oliver's head was thumping worse than before. Not from the camel kick, from the scrambled thoughts he was having.

If Mum and Dad hadn't lost Nancy's life savings, Rose's dad wouldn't have had to drill for water. And wouldn't have been killed.

No wonder Rose was so upset.

'Get the kid out of here before he bursts into tears,' Gail said to Nancy. 'Oh, and my hospitality's used up. I want you and Rose out of my place by tomorrow night.'

Oliver turned to Barclay, who was trembling on Erik's tummy and looking at Oliver with pleading eyes.

What would Dad do? thought Oliver.

He had a sudden urge to grab Barclay and run.

But it was two against four. Nancy was muscly, but she was small compared to Gail and the others.

And the others had guns.

Oliver gave Barclay a long look to show him he hadn't been abandoned.

Hang on, said Oliver silently. Don't bite anybody. I'll be back for you, I promise.

Then Oliver followed Nancy out of the house.

'That miserable cow,' said Nancy once they were outside. 'I shouldn't have dragged you into this.'

Oliver didn't reply.

He couldn't stop thinking about Barclay, still in that room with those guns and those smokers.

Oliver and Nancy got into the ute.

Nancy sat staring at the steering wheel.

'What a mess,' she said. 'I've got fifteen of Tim's camels a thousand k's from here, and if they don't get a drink this week, they're history. So at least now you can see why I've been behaving like a desperate mongrel.'

Oliver nodded.

He knew how she felt.

# 12

As the ute rumbled into the city, Oliver tried to stay calm. He went through the plan in his head.

Dad always said the best plans were simple and straightforward, and this was a beautifully simple nine-part plan.

(1) Tell Mum and Dad about Barclay being in big danger.

(2) Get Nancy to back it up with details.

(3) Introduce Moo to Mum and Dad.

(4) Tell them about the other camels.

(5) And Rose's father.

(6) Wait for them to be sympathetic.

(7) Ask them for money.

(8) Explain about it being an investment in the camel farm and not a refund.

(9) Use five hundred dollars of the investment to rescue Barclay, and the rest to save the camels.

Simple.

OK, ten parts, because first they had to take Moo to the bank, which they were doing now.

Oliver was squeezed in the front of the ute next to Rose. Every time Nancy took a corner, they were pressed together and Rose squirmed like she was being tortured by flesh-eating slime.

'Sorry,' murmured Oliver.

'Pig,' muttered Rose.

Oliver tried to be understanding. Rose didn't go to a normal school, she went to school on the internet, so she wasn't used to being near kids.

In the side mirror Oliver could see the reflection of Moo's float behind them. He almost wished he was back there with Moo.

Before they went round the next corner, Oliver tried to lighten the mood and take his mind off Barclay.

'Those camel biscuits,' he said to Nancy. 'What's in them?'

For a few moments it didn't look like Nancy was going to answer. Oliver could see she was still doubtful about the whole idea of taking Moo to the bank.

'We make them ourselves,' she said after a while. 'From leaves and twigs, ones that camels like, squashed together.'

Oliver knew how the leaves and twigs felt.

The ute went round another corner.

'Sorry,' said Oliver, pulling himself away from Rose.

'Don't speak to me,' Rose hissed.

She kicked Oliver. He gasped. Her boot was really hard.

'Rose,' said Nancy wearily.

Oliver rubbed his leg and tried to take his mind off the pain by thinking about what would happen when they got to the bank.

He was hoping Mum and Dad would come down to the foyer. Otherwise Moo would have to go up in the lift and Oliver was fairly sure that was illegal. Rose going up would be even worse. She'd probably set off the sprinklers or something.

'That one there,' said Oliver, pointing to the bank building.

Nancy parked outside and Oliver hurried into the foyer. While he waited for somebody to come down, he hoped Nancy wouldn't change her mind and drive off. Even as she was parking she'd still looked doubtful about the whole idea.

The lift doors opened, and Oliver started to have doubts himself.

It wasn't Mum or Dad in the lift, it was Hayden.

Hayden looked pale, like he was in shock.

For a second Oliver thought Nancy must have brought Moo into the foyer behind him, but before he could turn round to check, Hayden spoke.

'Your mum and dad have gone home,' he said.

Oliver stared at him. It was only four o'clock. Mum and Dad never went home at four o'clock in the afternoon.

'What's happened?' said Oliver.

Hayden looked like he didn't want to say. The lift doors started to close. Oliver had never seen Hayden like this. Scared and sort of helpless.

'Your parents'll tell you,' said Hayden, just before he disappeared behind the lift doors.

The closer they got to the apartment, the more anxious Oliver felt.

He knew now what must have happened.

He'd completely forgotten about Vickey picking him up from school. She must have called Mum and Dad when she found he wasn't there. Which was why they'd gone home earlier than they ever had in their lives.

His phone was probably full of angry messages from them.

Oliver couldn't check because his phone was in his school bag on the floor and he was still jammed in next to Rose.

They went round another corner. Oliver clung onto the door handle and tried not to touch Rose too much. But it was hopeless. Rose was like a hate magnet.

'I think I'm gunna throw up,' she muttered. 'Let's ditch this worm and go. This whole thing's a waste of time. Those murderers won't help us.'

Nancy didn't say anything.

Oliver felt even more stressed.

If Mum and Dad were angry with him, they

probably wouldn't want to help. And even if they weren't angry now, they would be after Rose had finished with them.

Oliver tried not to think about Rose getting her own back by scratching things in the apartment. Or letting Moo eat the giant bonsai trees in the foyer.

He had to risk it, for Barclay's sake.

'It's this block of apartments,' said Oliver, pointing.

'I know,' said Nancy. 'Remember?'

'Sorry,' said Oliver.

'You should be sorry, dung beetle,' said Rose. 'You couldn't afford to live in a flash block of flats like this if your parents weren't crooks.'

Oliver started to explain the difference between being a crook and having investment problems, using his own playground experience as an example.

Before he got very far, he saw something on the car-park ramp that made the words dry up in his mouth.

Vickey.

She was helping a taxi driver lift two big suitcases into the boot of a taxi.

Her suitcases.

Oliver scrambled out of the ute and ran over to her.

'Vickey,' he said. 'Where are you going?'

Even before she replied, he knew the answer from the look on her face.

'You could have texted me, Oliver,' she said. 'You

could have let me know where you were. So I didn't look like a complete dodo.'

Oliver tried to drag her suitcases out of the taxi.

'I'll explain to Mum,' he said. 'I'll tell her it was my fault. I'll explain you didn't know where I was.'

'Won't do any good,' said Vickey. 'Your mum's in a state. So's your dad. They were both home half an hour ago, furious you weren't here.'

'I'll explain to them,' said Oliver helplessly.

Vickey shook her head and gently took his hands off the suitcases.

Oliver knew she was right. It was hopeless. When Mum fired a housekeeper, she never changed her mind.

For a desperate moment Oliver wondered if a camel would change it.

No.

'I'm sorry,' he said miserably to Vickey.

'We both knew this would happen sooner or later,' said Vickey. 'I'll miss you.'

'I'll miss you too,' said Oliver.

Vickey opened the taxi door.

'It's not your fault,' she said. 'Your mum only fires us because she's jealous of us. Give me a call. Let me know what the next one's like.'

Oliver waved till Vickey's taxi turned a corner. He felt very sad, but at the same time his mind was racing.

What was going on with Mum and Dad? Why had they wanted him to be at home?

It must be something serious.

'She doesn't change, your mother, does she?' said Nancy.

Oliver turned.

Nancy and Rose were standing beside the ute.

Oliver took a deep breath.

'I'm really sorry,' he said. 'I think there's a problem. I think today's not a good day for Moo to meet Mum and Dad. Tomorrow would probably be better. Definitely better.'

'Garbage,' said Rose. 'You're a lying toad.'

'I promise,' said Oliver. 'Tomorrow will be much better.'

'Here's what you can do with your promise,' said Rose. 'Put it back up your bum where it belongs.' She turned to Nancy. 'We're not gunna get any help from this worm. Let me bash him with the jack handle, then we'll think of another way of getting our money.'

'Rose,' said Nancy wearily. 'In the ute, please.'

Instead, Rose came and stood very close to Oliver.

'When you're in bed tonight,' she said to him, 'and your servants are drying your toothbrush and bringing you a glass of water, have a little think about what's gunna happen to our camels in a few days.'

'Rose,' said Nancy. 'Get in.'

Rose scowled at Oliver and got into the ute.

Oliver looked at Nancy. He wished he could

say something to make her feel better. But until he found out what was happening with Mum and Dad, Rose was probably right, promises were risky.

'I'm sorry,' he said.

'Don't be,' said Nancy. 'You're a kid. I don't know what I was thinking.'

She reached into the ute and handed Oliver his school bag.

'I know you're fretting about the dog,' she said. 'But I've got sixteen camels to worry about.'

'I'll text you about tomorrow,' said Oliver.

'There may not be time,' said Nancy. 'Gail's chucking us out tomorrow afternoon and I have to get back to the farm.'

Nancy got into the ute, glanced up at Mum and Dad's apartment at the top of the building, and looked at Oliver through the open ute window.

'Looks like we're both in the poo,' she said grimly.

She drove off.

Oliver watched the ute go, but in his imagination all he could see was Barclay, trembling on Erik's lap, eyes pleading.

Oliver pulled himself together. There was still time to save Barclay and the camels. Tomorrow afternoon was twenty-four hours away.

Possibly more.

He hurried to the lift, and up to Mum and Dad.

# 13

'Where have you been?' said Dad, his voice loud with stress, as Oliver stepped out of the lift into the living room.

Oliver was expecting this.

For Mum and Dad to be home this early, they must have discovered how many school rules he'd broken.

(1)  Leaving the school premises without a note.

(2)  Catching a taxi without permission.

(3)  Selling shares in the playground.

(4), (5), (6)  Other rules, probably, that he'd forgotten.

Oliver decided not to make excuses or tell lies. A dog and sixteen camels were depending on him, so he had to tell the truth.

Which was what he tried to do.

'No, mate,' said Dad before Oliver had even got started. 'Haven't got time for this now. We've got to get back to the bank. All of us.'

Before Oliver could ask why, Mum hurried into the living room.

'Where have you been?' she said, 'We've been out of our minds with worry.'

Oliver was expecting this too. He started to apologise and explain, then stopped.

He looked at Mum, puzzled. She was wearing her faded business jacket that the dry cleaner ruined after Mum spilt champagne on it. And Dad was wearing a suit that looked about three years old. Usually he gave his suits to charity after twelve months. Six if they were silk and the elbows went baggy.

Oliver didn't get it.

What was going on?

He could see from Mum and Dad's faces it was something very serious. Even more serious than their son being a multiple school-rule breaker and a failed investment banker.

'What's going on?' said Oliver.

Mum and Dad looked at each other.

'I'll tell him,' said Dad.

Oliver had a horrible thought. Had Nancy and Rose gone to the bank and done something illegal with a jack handle? Were Mum and Dad wearing old clothes to clean up the mess?

'Walk and talk,' said Dad.

They all got into the lift.

'Here's what's happened, Oliver,' said Dad. 'A bank in America has just gone broke. All over the world, people are worried that other banks will go broke too. We don't want our investors to worry. We want to let them know that our bank is fine and their money is safe.'

'Because,' said Mum, 'if they think it isn't, they'll all ask for their investments back.'

'Today,' said Dad.

'And our share price will plummet,' said Mum.

'And we'll be in the poo,' said Dad.

Oliver thought about this as the three of them got into the car.

He imagined hundreds of angry investors, all with jack handles. He shuddered. He could see Ron the driver was looking nervous too.

'So,' said Dad as the car started moving. 'In thirty minutes we're holding a media conference.'

Oliver wasn't sure what that was.

'TV and radio and newspaper reporters are coming,' said Mum. 'We're going to explain to them that our bank is safe and sound.'

Oliver understood. It felt like a good idea. And once everybody had calmed down, then he could arrange for Nancy to tell Mum and Dad about Barclay and the camels and Rose's father.

There was one more thing about a media conference Oliver didn't understand.

'Why are you wearing old clothes?' he said to Mum and Dad.

They glanced at each other again.

'We want to show people we're just a normal

family,' said Dad. 'Working hard to look after everybody's investments.'

Oliver nodded.

Of course.

When people were feeling worried about losing their life savings, Mum and Dad didn't want to look too rich.

Oliver had never been to a media conference.

He didn't like it very much.

It was very hot, for a start. The boardroom was full of cameras and lights. Reporters were crowding and jostling.

Oliver sat between Mum and Dad at a table covered in microphones. He squinted into the lights. Sweat dribbled down his back.

'Can I take my blazer off?' he whispered.

'No,' said Mum.

'Yes,' said Dad. He leaned over and whispered to Mum. 'We don't want people to see he goes to a fat-cat school.'

Mum sighed.

The media conference began.

Oliver was shocked. The reporters were really rude. Instead of letting Mum and Dad explain how the bank was safe and sound, they kept yelling questions. Rude ones about whether Mum and Dad had been careful enough with people's money, and whether they'd told people the truth, and how much money they'd paid to themselves.

Poor Mum and Dad, thought Oliver.

Plus, the more the reporters were unkind, the more it made Oliver worry about whether Erik and his mates were being unkind to Barclay.

'Mr and Mrs Newton,' said a reporter, who looked to Oliver like a relative of the pet-shop manager because she had the same poodle hair. 'You say you didn't know you were putting your clients' money into investments that were time bombs waiting to explode in their faces. Did you ever actually explain to your clients the extent to which they were exposed to US subprime mortgage-backed derivatives?'

Oliver didn't have a clue what that question meant, but he could see that Dad wished the reporter hadn't asked it.

'I'm glad you asked that question,' said Dad, 'because it gives me the chance to remind everybody that this is an Australian bank, and we're doing just fine.'

Good one, Dad, thought Oliver.

Except Dad didn't look like he was doing just fine.

His knees were jiggling. Dad only jiggled his knees when he was very stressed. And Mum didn't look like she was doing fine either. Oliver could see her hands clenched tight under the table. Plus she was very pale, though that might just have been the dry-cleaning fumes from her jacket.

Oliver wished he could do something to help.

Mum and Dad must be wishing that too, he

thought, or why had they been so anxious for him to be at the media conference with them?

Oliver put up his hand.

'Can I say something, please?' he said to the reporters.

The room went silent. Everybody was looking at him. He stood up.

'Oliver,' whispered Mum urgently. She added something else he missed, but she was probably just wishing him luck.

Oliver's heart was going so fast he had a quick vision of it breaking and bits flying off, but he carried on.

'I just want to say,' he said to the reporters, 'that investment banking isn't easy. And anybody who thinks it is should give it a go, because then you'll see it isn't. Because nobody can be right all the time, not even people who are really good at maths. And when a bank like this one loses people's money, they don't mean to. That's all. Thank you for listening.'

Oliver sat down.

He was glad he'd taken his blazer off, because his school shirt was drenched with sweat.

Everybody was still staring at him.

He glanced at Mum and Dad. They were staring at him too. They didn't look like they were feeling much better than before, but he hoped they were on the inside.

Suddenly Oliver remembered something he'd

forgotten to say. He'd completely forgotten to remind everybody that the gone-bung American bank was probably very small and that Mum and Dad were too big too fail.

Before Oliver had a chance to stand up again and mention that, all the reporters started yelling questions. For a horrible few moments Oliver thought he'd have to answer them. But the bank public relations lady stepped forward and said in a loud voice, 'Thank you, thank you, no more questions, thank you.'

Dad grabbed one of Oliver's arms and Mum grabbed the other one and they steered Oliver out of the boardroom and along the corridor towards Dad's office.

Which was a relief.

Answering some of those questions would have involved maths.

Everybody was still hard at work in the trading room, talking urgently into phones and staring even more urgently at computer screens. As Oliver hurried past with Mum and Dad, he had a tiny hope that one or two of them might glance up and say, 'thanks for trying to help.'

Nobody did.

Oliver understood.

In investment banking you had to concentrate. Even taking the time to say thanks could cost you thousands of dollars.

Mum and Dad weren't saying thanks either.

Instead, they were muttering to each other over Oliver's head.

'You should have told him he was only there for decoration,' said Dad.

'I thought you'd tell him,' said Mum.

Oliver sighed.

Decoration, he thought miserably. Fail a few dozen maths tests and that's all people think you're good for.

It was his own fault. He'd completely forgotten to tell Mum and Dad about the A+ he got for his credit default swap project.

Oliver told himself to stop wallowing in self-pity. There were others worse off than him.

He tried not to think about what might be happening in a small house in the suburbs. A house with guns behind the TV. Where too much beer was probably being drunk. Except, Oliver remembered with a hopeful jolt, he'd heard somewhere that too much beer made people fall asleep.

Yes.

That's probably what was happening.

He imagined Erik and the other men asleep on the sofa and Barclay asleep in an empty beer carton.

Fingers crossed he was right.

And paws.

Oliver glanced up at Mum and Dad, who'd gone back to muttering to each other. You couldn't blame them for being stressed. Not after being bullied by those rude and unkind reporters, who didn't even ask about the incredibly long hours Mum and Dad worked.

Oliver squeezed both their hands to help them feel better.

Mum squeezed his.

'Thanks for trying to help, love,' she said.

Oliver glowed. And felt very tempted to ask them for five hundred dollars and a lift to the suburbs.

But he didn't. He could see how tense and distracted they still were.

Better to stick to the plan. Let them calm down, then let them meet Moo and hear Nancy's story from her own lips.

First thing in the morning, thought Oliver. As soon as Mum and Dad have relaxed and remembered they're too big to fail.

# 14

'Oliver, wake up.'

Mum was shaking him. Oliver peered at her, still half asleep. His eyes weren't fully working yet, but he could see that Mum's eyes were red and puffy, almost like she'd been crying.

Oliver sat up in a panic.

Had she been watching early-morning TV? A news story about a dog being treated unkindly in the suburbs? Or even worse, on an early-morning hunting trip?

'Oliver,' said Mum urgently. 'Come on, get up. We're going to the beach.'

Oliver stared at her, trying to make his sleep-wonky brain work properly.

The beach?

He peered at his watch.

Three-twenty.

Oliver blinked a few times to check if he was still asleep. No, he wasn't. It was actually happening.

Mum was dragging him out of bed at three-twenty in the morning.

'Get dressed,' said Mum. 'And put some clothes in a bag.'

She hurried out.

Oliver fumbled for his clothes. He knew he should be pleased. He'd been saying to Mum and Dad for ages he wished they could have a family holiday at the beach house.

But this didn't feel right. You didn't go on holiday at three-twenty in the morning.

Dad stuck his head into the room looking even more stressed than last night. His hair was sticking out as if he hadn't even had a shower.

'Only bring what you can carry,' said Dad, and hurried away.

Oliver tried to make sense of this. Why would you take something on holiday you couldn't carry? The beach house was fully furnished. There were beds and fridges already there.

Oliver shivered. This felt like one of those war movies where people had to get out in a hurry because planes full of bombs were coming.

Suddenly he had a horrible thought.

Nancy.

He didn't know her extremely well, but one thing was obvious. She desperately wanted to save her camels. And a person who could pretend to threaten a dog's life was capable of anything.

What if Rose had persuaded her to get tough?

To put some serious pressure on Mum and Dad?

Not with a jack handle.

With threats.

Bomb threats, for example.

As soon as Oliver got in the car with Mum and Dad, he knew his bomb-threat theory was totally silly. Whatever was going on here, it was much more serious than a bomb threat.

Dad was driving.

He never did that.

Oliver had been in the car with Dad heaps of times in his life, ten at least, and there was always a driver. It felt really strange now, being in the back by himself.

'Where's Ron?' said Oliver, as Dad steered the car out into the dark empty streets.

'Ron doesn't work for us any more,' said Dad.

Oliver waited for Dad or Mum to explain why, but neither of them did.

'Was he let go?' said Oliver.

That's how Mum always said it when she sacked a housekeeper. But it would be weird if Ron had been let go, because Dad never sacked drivers. Ron had been with them for as long as Oliver could remember.

'Was he?' said Oliver.

'That's enough,' said Dad angrily. 'Just be quiet.'

Oliver sank back into his seat, confused and worried. Dad hardly ever got this cross, except when things happened on the news to make share prices go down or wine prices go up.

'Pull over, Owen,' said Mum.

Dad kept driving.

'Please,' said Mum firmly.

Dad slowed the car to a stop outside a normal bank. Mum got out. For a moment Oliver thought she was getting some cash, but she wasn't. She slid into the back of the car next to him.

'Thanks,' she said to Dad.

Dad drove on.

Mum turned to Oliver.

Oliver couldn't remember ever seeing her this sad, not even a couple of days ago in her office.

'Ron doesn't work for us any more,' said Mum quietly. 'Nobody works for us any more.'

Oliver stared at her.

He mustn't have heard that right.

Mum put the armrest up and moved as close to Oliver as the seatbelt would allow.

'Oliver, love,' she said gently. 'I'm afraid there comes a time in every young person's life when they discover that the world isn't always a sweet and perfect place.'

Oliver was starting to feel sick. Not car sick. Frightened sick.

'What Mum's saying,' said Dad, not taking his eyes off the dark empty road, 'is that a terrible thing's happened and we're history.'

Oliver tried to see Dad's face in the mirror.

He couldn't. But he'd never heard Dad sound so miserable.

'A stupid, stupid thing,' said Dad. 'They had it all, those clowns in New York. Up to their armpits in wealth. Plenty for everybody, including us. But they blew it. They ruined it. And I trusted them.'

Oliver didn't understand.

'What clowns?' he said. 'Ruined what?'

'Everything,' said Dad.

Oliver's insides were tight with anxiety. Dad sounded like he was going to cry.

Mum squeezed Oliver's hand.

'The big banks in America,' she said, her voice almost as miserable as Dad's. 'Some more of them have gone broke. Their government is rescuing them.'

'Because they're too big to fail?' said Oliver.

'Yes,' said Mum, her voice almost a whisper. 'They are. But it turns out we're not.'

Oliver struggled to take this in.

It was something almost impossible to imagine.

'Has our bank gone broke?' he said.

Dad didn't reply.

Mum didn't say anything either. Just put her arms round Oliver and hugged him. He felt her tears on his face and knew the answer was yes.

The clanking of the automatic gate woke Oliver.

His neck was stiff.

Next to him, Mum was stretching and groaning.

We've arrived, thought Oliver.

He pulled the car curtains back and gazed at the big house where he'd had some of the happiest times of his life.

But not when it looked like this.

Oliver peered up at the dark windows, shocked.

Every other time he'd arrived, when he was little, the windows had all been blazing with lights. And people had been waiting at the big front door to welcome them. Cooks and maids and butlers, all nice people from the local agency.

Oliver stared at the silent empty house and remembered that everything was different now.

Sadly he wondered how big a bank or a beach house had to be before it was too big to fail.

The automatic gate was clanking closed behind them. Mum and Dad didn't seem to want to get out of the car. They were just sitting there, sort of stunned.

Poor things, thought Oliver. It must be really upsetting, thinking you're very good at maths and then discovering you're not.

Now that Oliver was in bed, he wanted to go back to sleep so he wouldn't have to think about things.

But he couldn't.

In the darkness outside his beach-house bedroom, the thud of the surf sounded like banks collapsing and injured animals plummeting onto grubby carpets.

Oliver crept out of his room to get a drink. As

he passed Mum and Dad's room, he heard them talking.

'What happens if they find it?' Mum was saying.

Oliver stopped and listened.

'They won't,' said Dad. 'It's all safe. Everything from our private accounts except the housekeeping one.'

'I heard at a conference that banks in Switzerland aren't as safe as they used to be,' said Mum.

Dad grunted, which sounded to Oliver like he didn't agree.

'What was the final figure?' said Mum.

'Can't remember exactly,' said Dad. 'The bank statement's in my briefcase. Just over thirty-eight, I think.'

'All our own money?' said Mum.

Dad gave another grunt, but this one sounded like a yes.

Neither of them said anything after that.

Oliver decided he didn't need a drink after all.

Back in bed, he quickly felt himself nodding off. The last thing he thought about was the number Dad had mentioned. He wished he could let Barclay and Nancy and Rose and the camels know the good news. Which was that when Mum and Dad said a number like thirty-eight, they usually meant thirty-eight million.

## 15

When Oliver woke up, sunlight was streaming into his bedroom. Outside, seagulls were squawking a welcome. Oliver rolled over sleepily and gazed out the big window. All the way to the horizon, the ocean twinkled.

Oliver's thoughts felt sunnier too.

OK, yes, life was going to be different. There'd be big changes. Bound to be when your parents had their own bank one day and didn't the next.

But it wasn't all bad news.

Mum and Dad wouldn't be so busy, for a start.

Then Oliver remembered Barclay.

Erik and his mates would be waking up soon, even if they'd had buckets of beer last night. And people who were cruel to animals were probably extra cruel first thing in the morning.

Oliver jumped out of bed. Time to talk to Mum and Dad about the thirty-eight million dollars in their bank account in Switzerland. And how just a small part of it could make a big difference to Barclay and the camels.

As Oliver opened his bedroom door, he heard a man sobbing.

For a second he thought it was Dad. But it didn't sound like Dad. Except Oliver couldn't be absolutely sure, because he'd never actually heard Dad sob.

Oliver hoped it wasn't Dad.

He went over to the gallery railing and peered down into the centre of the house. And gawked in surprise.

Down in the living area, sitting on one of the big white leather sofas, almost dropping an armful of office files as he tried to wipe his eyes, was Mum's assistant Hayden.

Mum and Dad were both standing in front of Hayden in their beach tracksuits, looking grim. Oliver wondered if he should offer to fetch Hayden a tracksuit so he could get out of his business suit and relax a bit.

'No bonus at all?' Hayden was saying. 'Nothing?'

'Sorry, mate,' said Dad. 'We're all in the same boat and it's sunk.'

'You told me I'd get four hundred thousand,' said Hayden, looking like he was about to start crying again. 'At the staff bonding weekend. You told me.'

'That was before all this,' said Dad.

'We're sorry, Hayden,' said Mum.

'You have to take those files back, mate,' said Dad to Hayden. 'If the authorities think we're trying to destroy bank documents, they'll have us on toast, mashed.'

Hayden sniffed and scowled.

'I was just trying to do the right thing,' he said. 'You're going to have investigators crawling all over the bank. Federal police, tax department, the lot. When you lose two hundred million dollars of your clients' money, people want revenge. They'll pin anything on you they can.'

'I know,' said Dad quietly. 'That's why we have to be out of the country by Monday morning.'

Oliver had started to go down the stairs. He stopped. His legs were suddenly so wobbly he didn't dare.

Two hundred million dollars?

Mum and Dad had lost two hundred million dollars?

Oliver sat down on the top step. He tried to calculate how many people that added up to. How many families like Nancy and Rose had trusted Mum and Dad with their money.

Hundreds?

Thousands?

Oliver couldn't work it out. The maths was too hard. So was the thought of how much human and animal suffering Mum and Dad had caused.

Down below, Mum was helping Hayden with his folders.

'Come on,' she said. 'I'll make you a cup of tea before you go.'

'Thanks for trying, mate,' said Dad to Hayden. 'But it's over. Take the files back, have a holiday, get another job, you'll be fine.'

'I've ordered a new BMW,' said Hayden bitterly. 'An M5. I'll lose my deposit now.'

Mum led him towards the kitchen.

Oliver went back to his room, got his school bag and made his way slowly down the stairs. His legs were still wobbly, but he had important things to talk to Dad about.

Dad was slumped on a sofa. Behind him, the ocean was glittering like a million of Mum's diamond earrings. But Dad wasn't looking at it. He was staring at a huge painting on the wall, the one of the bank buildings in New York silhouetted black against the setting sun. Dad had always reckoned one day he was going to have his own building right next to them.

Oliver remembered saying when he was little, 'Daddy, can you paint your one a happy colour?'

Now Oliver sat down next to Dad on the sofa.

'I was so sure I had everything covered,' Dad was saying, so quietly it was almost like he was talking to himself. 'Every collateralised debt obligation in our portfolio was hedged with a credit default swap. And every credit default swap was hedged with another credit default swap.'

Dad gave Oliver a sad smile.

'Sorry, mate,' he said. 'You don't know what I'm talking about, do you?'

Oliver shook his head. But it didn't matter

because there was something more important he wanted to say.

'Dad,' he said, 'I don't mind if we end up poor. We can live in a little house with a garden and grow our own veggies and have a dog.'

Dad frowned.

Oliver held out his bulging school bag.

'I can sell my iPad and PlayStation and stuff,' he said. 'To buy seeds and dog food.'

Dad put his arm round Oliver.

'Ollie, son,' he said. 'We're not poor. We've got plenty of money. Me and Mum have worked hard and we've saved lots. We'll be fine, mate.'

Oliver frowned. Dad was forgetting something really important.

'What about your customers who've lost all their money?' Oliver said. 'I know you won't be able to pay it all back, not two hundred million dollars, but you'll pay them what you can, right?'

Dad looked at Oliver.

'That's not how it works, Ollie,' he said. 'We're not a charity.'

Oliver stared at Dad, horrified.

'But, Dad,' he said. 'You've got thirty-eight million dollars. You can't just keep it.'

Dad was starting to look cross.

'Oliver,' he said. 'We're not going to give all our assets away and move into a hovel and live on turnips. I think it's best if you stop talking about things you know nothing about.'

'But I do know about it,' said Oliver, jumping to his feet. 'For a start, I know that if you're mean and selfish, an innocent dog's going to have horrible things done to him and sixteen camels are going to die of thirst.'

Dad glared at him, lost for words.

'What's all this?' said Mum, coming back in from the kitchen.

As fast as he could, before Mum and Dad had a chance to interrupt, Oliver told them about Barclay and Rose's father and the camels.

Mum and Dad stared at him.

Oliver could see they were shocked.

But then Dad stood up, shaking his head grimly.

'It's not that simple,' he said. 'Hundreds of our clients have lost their investments. If we start agonising about each one and giving them money, it's going to look like we've done something wrong. And we haven't. We've lost our bank. We're victims too.'

Oliver turned to Mum. She was looking more sympathetic.

'I know how you feel, love,' she said to Oliver. 'What's happened to Nancy's family is a tragedy. And they're not the only ones. I wish there was a way we could make it alright for everybody.'

Oliver was about to remind Mum there were thirty-eight million ways, but before he could her face went very weary.

'It's just not possible,' she said. 'We have other responsibilities. We have to think about you and your future. We have to put you first.'

'No you don't,' yelled Oliver. 'You have to pay people back. I don't want you to put me first. I don't want us to sneak off overseas. I want you to be generous and kind, not mean and selfish.'

Mum looked hurt.

Oliver didn't care, it was the truth.

'You're not being fair,' he yelled at them both. 'You're being selfish and sneaky.'

Dad looked like he was about to explode.

'Oliver,' he roared. 'Go to your room.'

Oliver hesitated. There was so much more he wanted to say. But he could see that talking wasn't going to make any difference.

Forget talking.

Mum and Dad had forgotten how to be generous and kind. It was up to him now, and this time he mustn't fail.

# 16

Oliver didn't feel good, hunting through Mum and Dad's bedroom.

He was a burglar in his own beach house. But he couldn't let Barclay and the others down. He had to find Dad's briefcase.

Suddenly Oliver saw it, tucked on top of the wardrobe. He dragged it down and clicked it open.

Nothing in the first compartment except an American investment magazine and a packet of tissues.

Oliver paused and listened.

Mum and Dad were still downstairs with Hayden. Dad was on the phone to the lawyers and Mum was offering to make Hayden a sandwich for the drive back and asking if he minded smoked oysters out of a tin.

The second compartment of the briefcase was full of sheets of paper.

Oliver flicked through them.

They were covered with numbers printed in neat columns. Some of the pages had other numbers written on by hand.

I need words, thought Oliver. In whatever language they speak in Switzerland.

He found some.

At the top of one of the sheets was the name of a bank that looked foreign. And under the name, other words that were definitely not English. And under the words, a list of numbers with a total at the bottom.

*$38,000,000.*

Yes.

Oliver grabbed his phone and took several photos of the bank statement, making sure he got all the numbers in.

He didn't feel like a burglar any more.

He felt like a spy.

But he didn't care.

Oliver wondered if paper cuts could kill you.

He didn't have any yet, but lying here in the back of Hayden's car covered with folders and print-outs and boxes of bank documents, he was definitely at risk. Once they were moving, if Hayden took a corner too fast, he could be slashed to ribbons.

Or was he just being silly?

Probably.

He wouldn't know for sure until Hayden stopped

arguing with Mum and Dad and got in the car and started driving back to the city.

Oliver could hear their voices.

'Blaming us won't change anything, Hayden,' Mum was saying. 'Just go please. When we find Oliver, we'll tell him you said goodbye.'

'I'll give that boy what for,' said Dad. 'When I send him to his room, that doesn't mean the beach.'

Come on, Oliver urged them silently. Time's running out. Camels are dehydrating and grumpy men with hangovers and guns are waking up.

At last Hayden got in the car.

Oliver held his breath. This was the risky moment. If Hayden decided to tidy up the piles of stuff in the back of the car before he drove off, Oliver was history.

But Hayden didn't.

As the car moved off, Oliver said a silent thank you to Hayden's mum, who had obviously let Hayden keep his room like a pigsty.

Oliver wondered if leg cramps could kill you.

They'd started ten minutes into the journey, and every time Oliver rubbed his legs he worried Hayden would hear him rustling under the folders.

Fortunately Hayden was playing loud music, a woman singing with a sob in her voice, and sometimes Hayden sang along with her and had a sob in his voice too. Other times he swore loudly about Mum and Dad.

Oliver found you could make leg pain a bit less painful by thinking about other things.

Rose, for example, and how unfair her life had been. And whether Mum and Dad had found the note he'd left in Dad's briefcase. And how Barclay was going.

Except worrying about Barclay was almost as painful as leg cramps.

Finally the car slowed down and joggled over some speed bumps.

At last, thought Oliver. We must be going down the ramp into the car park under the bank building.

Oliver had worked out what would probably happen next. Hayden wouldn't be able to carry all the files and documents in one go, so he'd probably go up in the lift and get a trolley.

After the engine stopped Oliver held his breath and listened.

He heard Hayden get out of the car.

Please, he said silently. Please don't let Hayden try to break the Olympic record for carrying paper.

Hayden didn't.

Oliver said a silent thank you to Hayden's dad, who obviously hadn't got Hayden interested in sport.

He counted to twenty-seven.

That should be long enough for Hayden to get to the lift.

Carefully, Oliver lifted the folders off his head and shoulders, eased himself up and peeked out the car window.

No sign of Hayden.

Oliver reached for his bulging school bag and hoped he hadn't made it too heavy for a quick getaway.

As Oliver hurried through the long grass to Erik's front door, he said a silent thank you to whoever invented phone maps and buses.

He did it silently because he was listening for Barclay.

A growl.

A whimper.

The crunch of a dog biscuit.

Any hint that Barclay was alive and well.

Oliver put his ear to the dirty peeling front door. He couldn't hear anything. He knocked, loudly.

And again.

And again.

At last he heard footsteps approaching through the house. Human ones, not dog ones.

The door opened.

Erik scowled at Oliver.

'I was asleep,' he said. 'What?'

Oliver gave him a friendly smile.

Erik didn't give him one back.

Oliver reminded himself what Dad always said about taking a chance and having a punt and risking it. Then he remembered he didn't want to be like Dad any more.

This is just me, thought Oliver.

'I've come for the dog, please,' he said.

Erik took off his glasses, polished them on his pyjamas, put them back on and gave Oliver a smirk.

Oliver was reminded of a look Dad used to get when he talked about tough deals he'd done at the bank.

'Five hundred bucks,' said Erik.

Oliver tried to look relaxed.

'So if I give you five hundred dollars,' he said to Erik, 'I can have Barclay. I mean that used second-hand dog?'

'You're quick,' said Erik.

They looked at each other for a while.

'I can do better than that,' said Oliver.

It was a phrase he'd often heard Dad use. But he was pretty sure Dad didn't invent it, which meant he could still use it too.

Oliver held out his school bag.

'Instead of five hundred dollars in money,' he said, 'I'll give you one thousand five hundred dollars in assets.'

Erik looked at the bag.

Oliver was about to explain what assets were, when Erik grabbed him by the shoulder and pulled him into the house.

While he was being steered into the dingy living room, Oliver kept his eyes and ears frantically open.

No sign or sound of Barclay.

Not a whimper or a wet patch.

'Show us what you've got,' said Erik.

The two other men from last time sat up in their armchairs and watched with sleepy interest.

Oliver crouched on the greasy carpet among the empty beer cans. From his bag he took his Xbox, his PlayStation, his iPad and his laptop and laid them out on the carpet in what he hoped was an attractive display.

'They're definitely worth one thousand five hundred dollars,' said Oliver. 'Easily. Even after depreciation for age and use.'

Erik looked at the other men.

'Shall we kill him and take his stuff?' said Erik.

The other men thought about this.

Oliver tried not to faint. Or run. In his pocket was his phone. He'd pre-dialled 000. He waited to see if Erik was serious.

The other men grinned and shook their heads.

Erik giggled.

Oliver was shocked. Even their jokes were cruel.

'OK,' said Erik to Oliver. 'I'm interested. What else have you got?'

Oliver desperately tried to think of a way to make his offer more attractive. Saying he'd also clean the bathroom was no good because he didn't have time. And he wanted to hang onto his noise-suppression headphones in case he and Barclay ended up living next to noisy neighbours.

'I'll throw in a pair of German binoculars,' said Oliver, taking them from his bag and putting them on the floor. 'They're really good for hunting small things like mice.'

The men in the armchairs frowned and Oliver realised he probably shouldn't have said that.

Erik was looking at all the stuff.

'Is it stolen?' he said.

'Do I look like a burglar?' said Oliver.

The other men snorted.

Erik held out a pudgy hand. Oliver shook it. Only one thing worried him. There was still no sign of Barclay.

Erik steered Oliver into the hallway and kicked open a door. Inside the room, lying on a dirty mattress with the expression of one who'd suffered much disappointment lately and had discovered that the world isn't always a sweet and perfect place, was Barclay.

'Take him and rack off,' said Erik. 'You can't have the lead cause I've lost it.'

Oliver didn't mind. All he cared about was having Barclay in his arms, which he soon did. And from all the wagging and licking and ecstatic panting that took place as they headed for the bus stop, Barclay was clearly a dog whose faith in life was totally restored.

# 17

As Oliver turned the corner into Nancy's street, he could hear Moo growling in the distance.

'OK,' he said to Barclay, who was sitting in his school bag. 'We're about to do something risky and possibly a bit illegal, and I'm afraid there are a couple of things you're probably not going to like.'

He turned the school bag round so Barclay was facing him and would pay attention and stop chewing the straps. It partly worked, though there was still a bit of chewing.

'First thing,' said Oliver. 'The camel. Try not to be scared, she's fairly friendly if you don't grab her rope.'

He decided not to mention anything about Moo kicking anybody in the head. No point making Barclay too anxious.

'Second thing,' said Oliver, and he knew this was going to be the tricky one. 'The girl. You've probably seen how sad and upset and a bit violent she is because her dad died.'

Barclay didn't try to jump out of the bag and run away, which Oliver thought was very brave.

'There is a third thing,' said Oliver. 'The woman with the knife is here too. She's had a tough time as well, so we have to try to be sympathetic. And with a loving pet like you around, who never kicks anybody in the head, I think she and the girl might both feel happier.'

Oops, he'd said the head thing.

'The important thing, Barclay,' added Oliver, 'is that I'll be with you at all times. And together we're going to help save sixteen camels, OK?'

Barclay licked Oliver's face, which suggested strongly to Oliver that it was OK.

In the driveway, the empty camel float was hitched to the ute. Luggage was piled up in the back of the ute and tied down with ropes.

'We got here just in time,' whispered Oliver to Barclay.

They squeezed past the ute, Barclay still in the bag. Oliver peered cautiously into the backyard.

Rose was there, gently rubbing ointment into a shaved patch on Moo's side. Oliver could see a long thin scar in the shaved patch with stitches crisscrossing it.

'Don't worry,' he whispered to Barclay. 'It was an operation. No stabbing was involved.'

Moo turned her head and saw Barclay and growled softly.

Barclay gave a yelp of alarm.

'It's OK,' Oliver whispered.

But it wasn't.

Rose turned as well and saw Oliver.

'Yuk, it's leech-boy,' she scowled. 'What are you doing here? Shouldn't you be hiding away with your criminal parents?'

Oliver knew this wasn't a time for arguments, but he couldn't stop himself.

'My parents aren't crooks,' he said.

Selfish, yes, but not crooks.

'Not crooks?' said Rose. 'So where did the four trillion dollars go, eh?'

Oliver stared at her.

Four trillion? Four thousand thousand million? If Rose thought that was how much Mum and Dad had lost, she must be even worse at maths than him.

'It was on the news this morning,' said Rose. 'Your parents have caused a global financial crisis.'

Oliver didn't know what to say.

He saw Nancy had come out of the house.

'Rose,' Nancy said wearily. 'We've been through this. Four trillion is what all the investment banks in the world have lost. Oliver's parents are only a tiny part of that.'

Oliver was relieved to hear it.

Nancy turned to him. She didn't look pleased to see him, but she didn't look angry either.

'You got the dog,' she said. 'Good on you.'

Oliver knew he didn't have much time, so he tried to be as clear and honest as he could.

'I'm here for two reasons,' he said. 'I mean three. No, two.'

Nancy sighed.

'First,' said Oliver, 'I want to say sorry on behalf of my parents. They'd probably say it themselves if their bank hadn't just gone broke.'

Before Oliver could go on to the second reason, Barclay scrabbled out of the bag, jumped down, trotted over to Rose and sniffed her feet.

'Yuk,' said Rose. 'Get your horrible dog away from me.'

Oliver sighed.

'Here, boy,' he said.

Barclay ignored him and started jumping and licking Rose's knees.

Rose bent down and picked Barclay up.

'Poor thing,' she muttered to Barclay, hugging him to her chest. 'Must be horrible having a worm for an owner.'

Oliver ignored her and turned back to Nancy.

'I'm also here,' he said, 'to make up for what Mum and Dad did, specially with Rose's dad dying and everything.'

'Come into the house,' said Nancy.

With an anxious glance at Barclay, Oliver grabbed his bag and followed her inside.

In the living room, newspapers were lying on the table and sofa. Oliver saw they all had headlines to do with banks going broke.

'Sit down,' said Nancy.

Oliver sat down.

Nancy stayed standing.

Oliver started to tell her more about the second reason he was here, but Nancy silenced him with a look. She picked up a newspaper.

'In the global investment playground,' Nancy read out, 'Owen and Rhoda Newton were a pair of first years.'

Oliver was shocked. That was a really unkind thing for a newspaper to write.

Nancy put the newspaper down.

'Your parents promised me a safe investment,' she said. 'I was probably dumb to believe them. But I was wrong to blame them for Tim's death. Tim was an adult who made his own choices and copped some tragic bad luck.'

She went silent and stared out the window.

Oliver was glad about what she'd just said, but he was nervous about interrupting again at such a personal moment. Though he was pretty sure Nancy was going to be pleased to hear the news he had for her.

'Jeez,' said Nancy. 'Look at that.'

Oliver stood up and peered out the window.

In the backyard, Rose and Barclay and Moo seemed to be getting on very well. Rose had put Barclay on Moo's back. The two animals were sniffing each other.

Rose was grinning.

'That's the first smile I've seen on her face in two months,' said Nancy.

Good on you, Barclay, thought Oliver.

He decided now was a good time to break the news to Nancy.

'I'm here to pay you back,' he said. 'And to give you a bit extra.'

'Extra?' said Nancy.

Oliver looked at the numbers he'd worked out on his phone calculator.

'Nine hundred and eighty-nine thousand dollars,' he said.

Nancy stared at him.

'Plus,' said Oliver, 'the eleven thousand dollars you invested, which makes a total of one million dollars.'

Nancy looked at him as if he was one hump short of a camel.

'Your parents have just gone broke,' she said.

Oliver took a deep breath.

'They've still got money,' he said.

He went to the photo of the foreign bank statement on his phone and handed the phone to Nancy.

She studied it. And swore under her breath.

'The mongrels,' said Nancy. 'They're keeping all this for themselves?'

Oliver nodded.

'They're keeping it for me as well,' he said. 'And

I give you permission to take a million dollars. The account number's there.'

Nancy stared at him.

She gave a snort.

'Doesn't work like that,' she said. 'A Swiss bank account has tighter security than a Wiggles concert. You can't just help yourself.'

Oliver could have booted himself up the bum. In his hurry to get away from the beach house, he'd totally forgotten to find out Mum and Dad's Switzerland pin number.

The sound of laughter came from outside.

Oliver and Nancy looked out the window again.

Barclay was standing on Moo's head, and Rose was laughing.

'What I wish I could help myself to,' muttered Nancy, 'is that dog. I should never have given him away.'

Then it hit Oliver. A way to make Mum and Dad do the right thing. A way that didn't involve any pin numbers at all.

'You can take Barclay to the farm if you like,' said Oliver. 'But you have to take me too.'

Nancy stared at him.

'Your parents'd have views about that,' she said. 'Strong views.'

'I left them a note,' said Oliver. 'They know I'm with you.'

Oliver admitted to himself that was a slight exaggeration. But it wasn't a lie. In the note he'd said he was going to see a housekeeper. He just hadn't said which one. There were nineteen possibilities and Nancy was one of them.

'Why would you want to go to the desert with us?' said Nancy. 'A woman who does desperate mongrel things and a girl who hates you.'

Oliver took a deep breath.

'Mum and Dad are planning to run away overseas,' he said. 'They can't if I'm not with them. Plus if I go with you, I think I can get your money.'

He looked at Nancy pleadingly.

She looked at him thoughtfully, then glanced out the window again at Rose and Barclay.

'I suppose I owe you,' she said. 'But you have to let those idiot parents of yours know exactly what's happening.'

Oliver grinned.

It was exactly what he was planning to do.

# 18

Oliver nodded awake.

Nothing had changed from the last time he'd woken up.

He was still in the front of the ute, speeding along the dark highway with Barclay snoring softly in his lap.

Next to him, Rose was still asleep, slumped against Nancy. Oliver wasn't surprised Rose was exhausted, the amount of time she'd spent whinging about him coming on the trip.

Nancy was still gripping the steering wheel, still staring at the road ahead, still looking like her thoughts were a thousand kilometres away.

They weren't happy thoughts, Oliver could see that. They probably involved burying camels.

Oliver looked at his phone to see if anything had changed there.

One thing had. The signal was even weaker than the last time he'd looked. But there was still no reply from Mum and Dad. Not a text or a voice message or anything.

For the squillionth time, Oliver checked the text he'd sent them to make sure it had actually gone.

*dear mum and dad*
*i'm with nancy*
*if you want me back pay her a million dollars*
*ring for details*
*oliver*

Yes, it had definitely gone.

Hours ago.

Mum and Dad must have got it by now. He'd sent it to both their phones, and left a voicemail.

Maybe they're having a long walk on the beach, thought Oliver. And maybe they've left their phones in the house.

Mum was always saying she wished they had more time to relax.

An hour later Oliver woke again.

He checked his phone.

Still nothing.

Why hadn't they replied? It was only eleven o'clock. Mum and Dad never went to bed before midnight.

'You won't get much of a signal this far out in the bush,' said Nancy, not taking her eyes off the road.

'I know,' said Oliver.

'Hope you sent a message to your dopey parents,' she said. 'So they know where you are.'

'Before we left,' said Oliver.

Rose wriggled in her sleep and grunted crossly, 'Mum, Dad, be quiet.'

Nancy glanced at Rose and stroked her head.

'Poor kid,' she said. 'Still dreams about her dad every night.'

Oliver didn't know what to say.

He stroked Barclay's head and tried to imagine what it would be like not to have a dad.

Or a mum.

He couldn't.

Gently, careful not to wake Barclay or Rose, Oliver put Barclay on Rose's lap. He didn't think Barclay would mind.

Then Oliver saw the screen on his phone was lit up. For a moment he thought it was a reply. But it wasn't. Barclay's paw must have touched the screen.

Oliver told himself to be patient. Mum and Dad wouldn't just ignore him.

There was one bar of signal left.

He wasn't giving up yet.


Six or seven or whatever hours later, Oliver gave up.

While Nancy and Rose and Barclay went for a walk up a hill, Oliver sat on a rock next to the ute, shoulders slumped, staring at the sunrise.

Along the vast rim of the outback horizon, dawn was creeping into the sky.

It reminded Oliver of an old TV ad for Mum

and Dad's bank. In the ad, the whole sky had turned gold, with big silver letters saying *We Care*.

This sky was starting to turn gold too. It was starting to look even more beautiful than the one in the ad.

Oliver wasn't interested.

He didn't want beautiful sights. He just wanted a message from Mum and Dad. But they hadn't sent one, and now his phone was out of range.

Oliver could hear the faint sound of Rose sobbing. She'd woken up crying for her dad, which was why Nancy had taken her up the hill. Oliver could also hear the soft murmur of Nancy's voice, comforting her.

He closed his eyes, trying not to think about Mum and Dad.

In a way, they had sent him a message.

*We Don't Care.*

It was what he'd feared, all the nights they'd worked late. A measly million dollars was more important to them than he was.

Suddenly Oliver heard something moving in front of him.

He opened his eyes. For a second he thought he was seeing things. A huge shape was blotting out the sky.

It was a shape Oliver recognised. He'd seen one like it yesterday on the front of a newspaper. A financial graph that looked like a big hump.

What was the shape doing here?

Oliver wondered if sadness could make you hallucinate.

Then the shape moved. And grunted. Big puddle eyes glinted in the gloom. Warm damp breath blew on Oliver's face.

It was Moo.

She was standing silhouetted against the dawn, looking at him.

Oliver jumped up in alarm.

Nancy had let Moo out of the float and tied some ropes loosely round her legs so she couldn't run off while she was eating bushes. She must have escaped.

Moo leaned towards him.

Oliver flinched. But then he felt her strong muscular neck gently rubbing his head.

It was nice.

'Thanks, Moo,' he whispered.

'Don't worry,' said a voice behind Oliver. 'She won't bite.'

Oliver turned.

Rose was coming down the hill, dress flapping in the breeze, boots kicking up clouds of dust. Nancy was next to her. Trotting close to them was Barclay.

'I know she won't,' said Oliver.

'I wasn't talking to you,' said Rose. 'I was talking to Barclay.'

She bent down and Barclay jumped into her arms.

'I need a nap in the ute,' said Nancy. 'Rose, can you get Moo back in the float, please.'

Oliver decided to go up the hill himself. Partly for a pee and partly to get away from Rose.

But Rose came over and stood in front of him, blocking his way.

'Mum told me how you used to visit Barclay in the shop window,' she said.

Oliver nodded, waiting for her to mock.

Rose looked down at Barclay for a moment, then squinted at Oliver.

'Thanks for sharing him,' she said.

Oliver blinked. When you hadn't had much sleep, your brain could play tricks. But Rose wasn't smirking or sneering.

'You're welcome,' he stammered.

'I only said that cos I'm sorry for you,' said Rose. 'Cos your parents have dumped you.'

Oliver started to say they hadn't, then stopped.

What was the point in defending them?

'My parents haven't dumped me,' said Oliver. 'I've dumped them.'

# 19

The roadhouse cafe was air-conditioned with tinted windows. Perfect for travellers seeking cool and shade after a long morning of highway heat and glare in a ute.

Oliver hardly noticed.

The only thing he was aware of was the TV on the wall. It was showing a news channel. He'd been staring at it for ages.

Nothing.

Not a single mention of a missing kid.

Oliver couldn't believe it. Mum and Dad hadn't even been to the police. It was twenty-nine hours since he'd left the beach house. No, twenty-seven. Well definitely over twenty, and they hadn't even reported him missing.

So this is what it feels like, thought Oliver. To be so sad and miserable you can't even eat.

When he was little he'd sometimes wondered how Mum felt when she let a housekeeper go. Did she feel stressed? Unhappy? Did she have so much sadness in her guts, she couldn't even swallow a toasted chicken schnitzel sandwich?

Probably not. Which just went to show what a big difference there was between letting a housekeeper go and letting your parents go.

'Do you want that?' said Rose, pointing to the piece of toasted chicken schnitzel sandwich on Oliver's plate.

'Rose,' said Nancy. 'Stop it.'

'I'm still hungry,' complained Rose. 'Half a sandwich wasn't enough.'

She pushed her wet thumb across the table and picked up a few crumbs from near Oliver's plate and put them in her mouth.

'Barclay's still hungry too,' she said. 'A growing dog can't survive on two chicken nuggets.'

On her lap, Barclay whimpered in agreement.

Rose leaned across the table again and got some more crumbs on her thumb and let Barclay lick them off.

'For pete's sake, Rose,' said Nancy. 'You know we need the rest of our money for petrol. You can eat when we get home. We've got sardines there.'

'I hate being poor,' muttered Rose.

Oliver pushed his half of the sandwich across the table to her.

'You have it,' he said. 'I'm not hungry.'

Rose grabbed the sandwich, tore it in two, ate one piece and gave the other to Barclay.

Oliver was wondering if she should have saved some for Moo and Nancy, when something caught his eye on the TV.

A photo of Mum and Dad.

'In financial news,' the newsreader was saying, 'failed bankers Owen and Rhoda Newton are today under investigation.'

'Jeez,' said Rose. 'Is that them?'

There was a shot of the beach house. Oliver was horrified. The beach house was meant to be secret, so Mum and Dad could have a break from work when they needed it. Only employees knew about it.

Hayden must have dobbed them in.

'The whereabouts of the high-flying couple is unknown,' continued the newsreader. 'Authorities say it's too soon to determine whether the Newtons will face criminal charges.'

Oliver stared at the TV screen, not seeing it any more.

He shivered.

The air in the roadhouse suddenly felt freezing.

He stood up.

'Oliver,' said Nancy.

'I need to go to the toilet,' said Oliver, and ran.

What he needed was somewhere to think. He locked himself in a cubicle and sat down on the toilet lid.

Criminal charges?

Oliver struggled not to panic.

Mum and Dad weren't criminals. Only angry people like Rose thought they were criminals.

Luckily there weren't many like her. Well there were actually. Oliver tried to calculate how many. All of Mum and Dad's customers basically. Two hundred million dollars' worth. What if a judge listened to them all? Dad would be a broken man in jail. Mum would hate it. The violence and the loneliness, plus there was nowhere to store shoes.

Calm down, Oliver told himself.

Try to think clearly.

At least now I know why Mum and Dad haven't contacted me. They're on the run. But where?

He knew you couldn't leave the country if the cops were after you. There'd be photos at all the airports. And dogs.

Oliver's mind went into a blur, trying to imagine what Mum and Dad were doing.

Then, after a while, he had a clear thought.

Sometimes you had to dump your parents for a while if they were being mean and selfish. But you didn't leave them dumped if things got really bad.

Not when they really needed you.


The roadhouse supervisor's office smelled of grease from cars.

Oliver could see some of it smeared on the screen of the supervisor's old-fashioned computer.

It didn't matter.

All that mattered was that the roadhouse had

internet and the supervisor was letting him send an email.

'Five minutes,' said the supervisor, pointing to the torn vinyl chair in front of the computer.

Oliver was tempted to try for a better deal. He was pretty sure that even in these parts, a pair of noise-suppression headphones should get you more than five minutes of non-WiFi internet access and three packets of gingernut biscuits.

The supervisor was looking impatient.

Oliver decided not to bother.

He ignored the grease on the chair, sat down, and unfolded the rego papers he'd borrowed from the glove box in the ute.

Five minutes would be long enough. It didn't need to be a long email. Just the address of Nancy's farm. At least then Mum and Dad would have somewhere to hide out from the law.


Quickly, so nobody would see him, Oliver put the rego papers back into the ute glovebox. Then, gingernut biscuits under his arm, he hurried back into the roadhouse cafe.

And stopped.

Over at the table, Nancy and Rose were arguing.

'Do you know the penalties for kidnapping?' Rose was whispering loudly and angrily. 'Life in prison probably.'

'It's not that bad,' said Nancy. 'You've been watching too much TV.'

Oliver frowned.

Kidnapping?

Then he saw what was on the table in front of them. His phone. He must have left it there when he rushed out.

Had they seen his text to Mum and Dad, the one about the million dollars? Which, Oliver had to admit, did look a bit like a kidnapping demand.

'The police use roadblocks to catch kidnappers,' Rose was saying.

Nancy stood up.

'Break over,' she said. 'Time to make a move. I want to get to the farm.'

Oliver hurried across. He was about to offer to send Mum and Dad an email telling them he definitely wasn't being kidnapped, when Nancy put a hand on his shoulder.

Ouch.

Her grip was really powerful.

'Come on, Oliver,' she said. 'We don't want to lose you.'

Rose picked up Barclay, and Oliver just had time to grab his phone before Nancy steered him towards the exit.

As they stepped out into the blinding heat, Oliver wondered if he should explain about the kidnapping misunderstanding.

Then he had another thought.

A scary one.

What if seeing the text had given Nancy an idea?

What if she'd thought of a way to definitely get the million dollars? A way that explained her grim face and the very tight grip she had on Oliver's shoulder.

Oliver remembered how when Nancy was desperate, she did desperate mongrel things.

What if he was really being kidnapped?

# 20

'This driving's making me feel a bit brain-weary,' said Nancy. 'So I'll leave the maths to you.'

'Sorry?' said Oliver.

He'd been deep in thought about other things. Wondering if Mum and Dad would send his text to the police. Wondering if the police would set up an anti-kidnapping roadblock. He'd also been looking at Rose asleep with her arms round Barclay and wondering if he was ever going to get Barclay back.

'I'm worried we haven't got enough fuel to get to the farm,' said Nancy.

Oliver stared at her.

'I see I've got your full attention at last,' said Nancy.

She certainly did.

This shimmering strip of bitumen stretching ahead of them was the loneliest road Oliver had ever seen, even in movies. They'd been driving for hours and they'd only seen three other cars.

Get stranded here, thought Oliver, and it doesn't matter if you're being kidnapped or not. The poor camels at the farm wouldn't be the only ones dying of thirst and hunger.

Oliver wished he and Nancy and Rose and Barclay and Moo hadn't eaten all the gingernuts.

'Here's the maths,' said Nancy. 'We're about a hundred k's from the farm. Fuel gauge says quarter of a tank, which is about eighteen litres, except the gauge is faulty, so I'm guessing about half that. Loaded up like this and pulling a camel, we're doing about seven k's to the litre owing to the ute not having been serviced for a year. What I want you to work out is, are we going to make it?'

Oliver felt the familiar grip of maths panic.

He fumbled for his phone, praying he had enough battery left to work the calculator. Before he could check, Nancy spoke again.

'Don't bother, I've just worked it out.'

Oliver sighed with relief.

'We're not going to make it,' said Nancy.

Oliver stared at her again.

'Which is why we have to turn off somewhere along here,' she said. 'There's a dirt side-road, a short cut. Bumpy, but it'll save us forty k's. Trouble is, I haven't used it for years. Can't remember which turning it is.'

Oliver switched on his phone to see if he could get Google maps.

He couldn't.

'OK,' said Nancy, 'here's the harder maths. I know the turning is eighty-nine k's from the Cooper's Corner intersection we passed a while back. And these posts on the side of the road with the reflectors on them, they're meant to be one every kilometre.'

Nancy pointed, and Oliver saw a post as they whizzed past it.

'But,' said Nancy, 'the bloke who put them in was having a fight with the Department Of Main Roads about some overtime he hadn't been paid, so he put the posts in every twelve hundred metres instead. I've been counting posts since the intersection. We've just passed number sixty-five. What I need you to work out is, how many more posts till our turn-off?'

Oliver felt the maths panic coming back.

How many lots of twelve hundred metres in eighty-nine kilometres?

He didn't have a clue.

'I know,' said Oliver. 'Why don't you just use the odometer on the dashboard to measure the distance?'

'It's broken,' said Nancy.

Oliver felt sick.

He switched on his phone again and tapped the calculator.

The battery went dead.

'Sixty-seven,' said Nancy. 'We just passed the sixty-seventh post.'

'We've missed the turn-off,' said Oliver in a panic.

'How can you know that,' said Nancy, 'until you do the maths?'

Frantically, Oliver tried to do the maths. The numbers immediately got jumbled in his head. If only Mum and Dad were here, they could do it.

Oliver stared out the window at the desert sky. Perhaps Mum and Dad would come to the farm by plane and perhaps they'd fly overhead and he could wave to them and they'd land on the road up ahead and . . .

'Post number sixty-eight,' said Nancy.

Oliver closed his eyes and tried to concentrate.

'Take your time,' said Nancy. 'But try to get it right, because if we overshoot we'll burn up even more petrol.'

Oliver felt Barclay licking his hand to encourage him. And slowly, slowly, the numbers fell into place. He checked them in his head. They stayed in place.

'Seventy-two,' said Oliver. 'We turn at post number seventy-two.'

'We just passed number seventy,' said Nancy.

Oliver held his breath for the next two-point-something kilometres. Or two posts as he preferred to think of it.

'Number seventy-two,' said Nancy.

Oliver stared through the insect-spattered windscreen. Where was the turning?

They passed another post. And another.

Oliver was about to suggest to Nancy she'd got her counting wrong. Then she slowed the ute and Oliver saw black tyre marks on the road ahead curving into a dirt side-road.

'Yes,' he shouted.

'What?' mumbled Rose, waking up.

Nancy steered the ute and the camel float off the highway onto the dirt road.

'It's very narrow,' said Oliver. 'The police probably wouldn't bother putting a roadblock on a track like this.'

Nancy didn't reply.

Oliver realised he probably shouldn't have said that out loud.

A little while later, Oliver decided to confess about the email he'd sent.

He had two reasons.

OK, three.

'Nancy,' he said. 'Back at the roadhouse I sent an email to Mum and Dad saying they could hide out at your farm. Sorry I didn't ask you first.'

Oliver waited anxiously for Nancy's reply.

He hoped she wouldn't be angry, but he was glad he'd admitted it because:

(1) it was polite.

(2) he'd be able to see if Rose was planning to attack Mum and Dad on sight.

(3) it might give him a clue about whether he was being kidnapped.

Nancy just grunted, and Rose just muttered something about dung weevils.

Oliver sighed.

He had a horrible feeling that was yes to (2) and (3).


Rose wasn't a very good singer, but that didn't stop her.

'Ten green bankers,' she sang, 'sitting on the wall. If one green banker should accidentally fall . . . come on, dropkick, you're not singing.'

Oliver joined in, but only because now it was dark Nancy said she needed singing to keep her awake.

'. . . there'd be nine green bankers sitting on the wall.'

Oliver wasn't enjoying this part of the trip. For a start, Rose got to choose the songs. Plus this dirt road was very bumpy. The sloshing from the water tanks on the roof was so loud Oliver was worried they were going to fall off. He hoped the bumping wasn't too painful for Moo in the float.

He didn't even want to think about what would happen when they got to the farm.

What if Mum and Dad didn't turn up because they'd been arrested? What if they did turn up, but without any kidnap money?

'You two,' said Nancy. 'Keep your eyes out for wildlife.'

'If we hit a roo, it won't be pretty,' said Rose, sounding as if she didn't mind the idea.

Oliver peered into the dusty headlight beams. Ahead of them, the dark desert was full of weird shapes. Any one of them could be alive. Mostly the headlights revealed them to be just bushes or rocks, but until then any one of them could be a kangaroo or a crouching police sniper.

Rose held Barclay up so he could see out the windscreen.

'Dogs have amazing night vision,' she said.

Oliver hoped Nancy's night vision was amazing too. He glanced at her. In the dull light from the dashboard she was looking tired and not as stern as usual.

Suddenly Oliver couldn't stand it any more.

The stress of not knowing if he and Barclay were prisoners.

He decided to get it over with.

'Nancy,' he said. 'Am I being kidnapped?'

Nancy gave him a sharp look. Before she could say anything, Rose screamed.

'Mum,' she yelled. 'Look out.'

Oliver, startled, peered out the windscreen. There was something ahead of them, at the bottom of a long sloping stretch of the road.

Was it a roadblock?

No, it was a wide riverbed.

'Jeez,' said Nancy. 'That shouldn't be there.'

'It's OK,' said Oliver. 'It hasn't got water in it.'

'That's worse,' yelled Nancy.

They were skidding now and Rose was screaming

again and Barclay was barking and they weren't stopping.

'Hold on,' yelled Nancy.

Oliver grabbed Barclay and the ute hit the sand and then it was terrible.

# 21

Finally the ute stopped rolling.

It was dark. And quiet. Oliver's chest hurt. Bodies seemed to be piled on top of him.

Oliver heard a whimper from Barclay. He reached out, trying to feel if Barclay was alright.

Rose groaned.

'Barclay,' she croaked. 'You're OK, I've got you.'

Oliver could feel Rose's weight on him. Something was jammed into the side of his head. It was hard, like a knee.

Nancy groaned in the darkness. She sounded like she was in pain.

'Rose,' she said. 'Are you alright?'

'I think so,' said Rose. 'My head might be bleeding a bit.'

'What about you, Oliver?' said Nancy.

Oliver was about to say that his chest hurt a lot, but then he realised what might be causing it. He felt around for his seatbelt buckle. When he pressed it, the buckle slipped away from his chest and the pain went almost immediately.

'I'm OK,' said Oliver.

'Come on,' said Nancy. 'We need to get out.'

Slowly, with difficulty, they clambered out. Nancy went first because she was on top. While Rose followed her, Oliver held Barclay, who was trembling even more than he was. Then Rose took Barclay, and Oliver dragged himself out through the window, which seemed to be in a different place to usual.

Nancy, squinting in the moonlight, was examining Rose's head.

'I'll live,' said Rose.

'It's just a cut,' said Nancy. 'Not deep. Oliver, you're sure you're OK?'

'Yes, thanks,' he said.

He was more concerned about Barclay.

Oliver picked Barclay up and checked him over for injuries before giving him a relieved cuddle.

Nancy staggered and almost fell over.

'Mum,' said Rose, grabbing her. 'What's wrong?'

'My ankle,' said Nancy. 'It got twisted under the brake pedal.'

Oliver and Rose helped Nancy flop down onto the sand. Then Oliver looked at the wreckage all around them.

The ute was on its side. One of its wheels was off. Luggage was scattered around. The big plastic water tanks were split and empty.

'Where's Moo?' said Rose in alarm.

Oliver realised the camel float wasn't hooked up to the ute any more. He couldn't see it anywhere, not in the riverbed, not in the scrub.

'This is crazy,' he said. 'It can't just have –'

Rose grabbed his arm and put her finger to her lips.

They listened.

No camel noises.

Nothing.

'Moo,' yelled Rose frantically. 'Moo.'

Oliver heard a growl.

But it wasn't Moo. It was Barclay, crouched by their feet, tail stiff, peering into the shadows.

He started barking and ran off along the riverbed.

'Come on,' said Rose, running after him.

'Be careful,' called Nancy.

Oliver followed Rose and Barclay, sprinting into the darkness. The soft sand made running difficult and the moonlight was patchy so he had to be careful not to bash into things.

Like this big chunk of the camel float, lying upside down. It seemed to be the top part, torn from the chassis like a big empty smoked-oyster tin.

Oliver stopped. He winced as he imagined what might have happened to poor Moo. He didn't want to go on. Didn't want to see . . .

Then he heard Rose yell.

He hurried on.

There was Moo, lying on the sand, not moving.

Rose was kneeling and stroking Moo's head and moaning. Barclay was sniffing Moo's long graceful neck, his ears flat and his tail down.

Oliver hurried over and joined Rose. He slid his hands gently over Moo's woolly fur, hoping he wasn't hurting her, checking her big body for injuries.

All he could find were a few cuts. The stitches from her operation were all still connected.

But Moo's eyes were closed and she definitely wasn't moving.

Rose let out a wail.

Oliver tried not to think about poor Moo being flung out of the float, her heavy body crashing into the ground, something snapping inside . . .

'Moo's dead,' sobbed Rose.

Oliver put his arms around Rose. He felt like crying himself, but he managed not to. Until he thought about Rose, who'd lost two members of her family now, which was more sadness than any person should ever have to bear.

Then he almost did cry. Until he heard a gurgling-spluttering sound. Sort of like vomiting.

He looked down.

Thick mucus stuff was coming out of Moo's mouth.

'Rose,' said Oliver. 'Look.'

Moo was coughing the stuff out.

They stared as Moo spluttered and gurgled

until there was a puddle in the sand. Then slowly, struggling and trembling, she rolled onto her tummy, knees tucked under her.

'Moo,' whispered Rose.

It took Moo a long time to stand up, but she did it, back legs first, then front. Rose put her arms round Moo's neck and hugged her.

Oliver realised he was shaking.

He picked up Barclay, who was jiggling like a blender on high.

'I think she's OK,' said Rose, running her hands under Moo's belly.

Moo leaned forward and rubbed Rose's face with hers. Rose wiped a blob of mucus off her own chin, took Barclay from Oliver, and lifted him onto Moo's back.

Oliver watched them.

If I was a camel or a dog, he thought, and a bunch of humans had made me be in a crash, I'd be really upset. I'd be grouchy and complaining and trying to bite them or kick their bums.

But Barclay's tail was wagging and Moo was just standing there, her body trembling only a bit now, her friendly mouth in a sort of half-smile, her big placid eyes looking like they'd seen it all before.

After Nancy finished checking Moo herself, leaning for support on Oliver and Rose's shoulders, she decided they should all get some sleep and wait for daylight.

'Try to find the swags,' she said.

Oliver wasn't sure what a swag was. He soon saw as he helped Rose drag one from under the twisted tailgate of the ute. It was like a big sleeping bag, quilted on the inside and waterproof on the outside.

There were three swags.

Rose and Oliver laid them out side by side on the sand, and helped Nancy wriggle painfully into one. Rose got into the middle one with Barclay.

Oliver stood by the third swag. He wasn't sure what he should do.

'Sleep in a tree if you prefer,' said Rose.

'Isn't this your dad's?' said Oliver uncertainly.

Even if your parents weren't responsible for a person's death, you didn't just jump into his swag.

'He doesn't use it any more,' said Rose quietly.

'Get in,' said Nancy.

Oliver got in.

'Here,' said Rose. 'In case you get scared of the dark.'

She handed Barclay over.

'Thanks,' said Oliver as Barclay snuggled into the swag with him.

It was a good feeling, lying there, staring up at the squillions of stars and listening to Moo's soft breathing and Barclay's panting. As long as you didn't think about where you were, and why, and whose fault it was.

'Nancy,' said Oliver quietly. 'It was the wrong road, wasn't it?'

'Yup,' said Nancy.

'Sorry,' said Oliver. 'I'm really bad at maths.'

'Wasn't your maths,' said Nancy. 'It was my fault. I thought I recognised the turning and I got it wrong.'

Oliver didn't understand.

'That stuff about the posts,' said Nancy. 'I made it up.'

Oliver was even more confused.

'You talk in your sleep, idiot,' said Rose.

'You mumble about maths tests,' said Nancy. 'Which apparently you always fail. You sound pretty stressed about it. So I thought I'd give you a chance to get some maths right for a change.'

'So at least somebody in your family does,' said Rose.

Oliver took a few seconds to digest this.

'So those posts didn't really have anything to do with where the turning was?' he said.

'No,' said Nancy.

'Der,' said Rose.

'And I got the maths right?' said Oliver.

'I didn't say that,' said Nancy.

Oliver felt his insides droop.

'There are more important things in life than maths,' said Nancy quietly. 'Including what you did for Rose a little while ago.'

'Can we go to sleep now?' said Rose.

In the darkness, Oliver gave Nancy a grateful look.

'One more thing,' said Nancy. 'The answer's no.'

It was the answer Oliver had been hoping for.

'We don't kidnap people,' muttered Rose. 'Even when we do see something stupid on their phone.'

Oliver snuggled into his swag and cuddled Barclay.

He felt even better than before.

As long as he didn't think about Mum and Dad and whether he'd ever see them again.

# 22

When Oliver woke up, the sun was already hot.

He reached for the remote control to turn up the air-conditioning, then remembered where he was.

In a swag with Barclay.

Lost in the desert with Nancy and Rose.

Oliver tried not to panic. He tried not to think about anybody wandering desperately around in circles and dying of thirst.

As he and Barclay crawled out of the swag, Oliver tried to do what Dad often said. Think about the best that could happen today, not the worst.

Oliver knew what the best would be. Everybody safe, and Mum and Dad not in jail.

Barclay helped.

Which was kind. It was easy to think positively when a good friend was licking your face.

'Thanks,' said Oliver.

Then he saw that Nancy and Rose were both awake and looking anxious.

'Moo's wandered off,' said Nancy.

'I hobbled her really tightly,' said Rose. 'She must have been really desperate to get away.'

Nancy's ankle was so swollen she couldn't even stand up, so Oliver went with Rose and Barclay to look for Moo.

It took a while.

They found her, a long way from the road, ropes still round her legs, chewing a bush.

'I don't get it,' said Oliver. 'These bushes are everywhere. Why did she come so far for this one?'

'Don't be an idiot,' said Rose. 'She didn't come this way for a feed. She's trying to get home. Camels always do that. They can find their way home from anywhere.'

Moo was gazing at the horizon.

'Our farm must be that way,' said Rose.

Oliver gazed too. All he could see between them and the horizon was about a squillion kilometres of flat scrubby desert.

Without any roads.

When they got back to the riverbed, Nancy agreed that Moo had been trying to head home.

'So we know which way to go now,' she said.

But Nancy still couldn't stand up. And the ute was crippled too. As well as missing a wheel, the front axle was broken.

Oliver and Rose tried to lift Nancy onto Moo's back.

Moo was very patient, but after a lot of heaving and straining by Oliver and Rose, and a lot of swearing by Nancy, they had to accept it wasn't going to work.

'Thanks for trying,' said Nancy. 'Don't know if I could have stayed up there for long without a saddle anyway.'

Oliver and Rose helped her flop back against the side of the ute.

'You two go with Moo,' said Nancy. 'When you get to the house, radio for help. I'll wait here.'

'No,' said Rose. 'I'm not leaving you.'

Oliver could tell from her face what she was really saying.

I'm not risking losing you as well.

'I'll go,' said Oliver. 'Moo will show me the way. I can come back with my parents in their car.'

Rose snorted.

'You on your own with a camel?' she said. 'You'd get about half a k.'

'Anyway,' said Nancy, 'what if your parents aren't there?'

'Yeah,' said Rose. 'What if they've nicked off to Switzerland? That's the sort of low, selfish thing they'd do, right?'

'No need for details, Rose,' said Nancy.

Oliver turned and ran along the riverbed, Barclay at his heels.

Behind him he heard Rose say, 'No need for tantrums either.'

Oliver wasn't having a tantrum. He just didn't want to think about Switzerland. He'd rather think about a best thing, which was Nancy getting some transport.

Yes, there it was, just as he'd hoped.

In the riverbed, near the torn-off top half of the camel float, was the bottom half. And it looked all in one piece. The wheels were still on it, and the axles between them seemed fine. Even the carpet was in place.

There was jagged metal around the edge, though, which would have to be dealt with so Nancy didn't get stabbed. And they'd have to find some way of attaching a tow-rope.

Oliver wished he was better with tools.

Rose was very good with tools.

With a pair of pliers she made the jagged metal less jagged, and twisted some of it into a loop they could tie a rope to. Soon Nancy was lying on her new transport, cushioned by the carpet and all three swags.

Oliver and Rose gathered up the other things they were taking with them.

Which weren't many. Nancy was very strict about keeping the weight down. Just a couple of suitcases and some hats and sunblock and some cough lollies from the glovebox, which was the only food they had. Plus the only unbroken water container, which was a human-sized one with about four litres of water in it.

Oliver added his school bag to the load. Nobody seemed to mind. They must have known it was Barclay's favourite thing.

Then it was time to set off.

As Rose looped the tow-rope around Moo's shoulders, and tucked towels under it so it wouldn't rub her skin, Oliver had a moment of anxiety.

Even without a top and without much luggage, half a float was a heavy thing for one camel to tow. Specially a camel who was recovering from an operation and a car crash.

Oliver threw himself behind the float and gave it a push to help Moo get started. He pushed with all his strength.

The float didn't move.

Then Moo started plodding forward, the rope tightened, and they were off.

# 23

The horizon danced away from them in the heat.

Oliver soon gave up pushing the float. He wasn't making any difference and he wanted to save his strength in case Moo collapsed from exhaustion and he and Rose had to put the rope round themselves and haul Moo and Nancy home.

So far Moo was plodding at a steady pace, moving across the desert like an elegant ship, but with a big friendly mouth at the front instead of old tyres.

Oliver hoped she knew where she was going.

The desert seemed to go on forever.

Millions of dry bushes.

Billions of sharp little rocks.

Trillions of scurrying ants.

Barclay raced around sniffing at the ants for a while, but got too hot and jumped up with Nancy.

Lucky thing, thought Oliver.

The heat was terrible.

Everything was shimmering, including the inside of Oliver's head.

He was tempted to ask if they could take a break, but he didn't. Rose was plodding along leading Moo without any complaining. Anyway, what was the point. There wasn't any shade.

'Are we there yet?' said Nancy after an hour or two. Or three. With his phone battery dead, Oliver had lost all track of time.

He glanced at Nancy, worried that perhaps she was going delirious in the heat. They were clearly not there. The farm wasn't even in sight. It might be in a different state, for all Oliver knew.

Rose held up the water container for Nancy to see. It only had a small amount of water left in it.

Oliver realised what Nancy had meant. All morning she'd been making sure everybody had a regular mouthful of water. Though Oliver had noticed her own swigs were tiny.

She'd been asking if they'd run out yet.

Which they almost had. There was just enough for one more mouthful each, including Barclay.

'What about Moo,' said Oliver after he'd had his.

'She's fine,' said Nancy. 'She filled up back at the roadhouse.'

Oliver struggled with his heat-affected memory. Had they passed a roadhouse today that he'd missed? He didn't think so. Not unless it had been behind an ants' nest.

He realised what Nancy meant.

The roadhouse yesterday lunchtime.

'She'll be fine for a couple more days,' said Nancy.

'She did have seventy litres,' said Rose. 'And a lemonade.'

Oliver plodded along beside Moo, impressed. He looked at the way her slender legs and powerful body kept the float wheels turning over the bumpy ground. It didn't look like any effort at all, but Oliver was pretty sure it must be.

After a while he noticed a part of her back that was like a sort of ledge, just behind her hump. He imagined perching up there and having a snooze, just a quick one . . .

'Thinking of having a ride?' said Rose.

Oliver gave her an embarrassed look and waited for a hurtful remark.

All she said was, 'You can if you want. But only tourists ride. In this family when we trek camels, we walk with them.'

Oliver thought about this.

'Want a leg up?' said Rose.

'No thanks,' said Oliver. 'I'm fine.'

And he was.

Doing it the way it was done.

In this family.

# 24

And then it was just plodding.

Very hot plodding.

Oliver stopped peering ahead. He didn't want to see that the farm still wasn't in sight.

As he plodded he kept his eyes down, focussed on Moo's feet as they padded across the desert, keeping the float wheels moving steadily, never speeding up, never slowing down, a rhythmic plod he was grateful to have guiding him on.

Oliver started thinking about plodding.

Plodding had a bad name. In maths at school Mr Langrish was always accusing him of plodding, like it was a crime or an illness.

People who plodded were reckoned to be a bit thick, or boring, or not very original, or a joke.

Well that's wrong, thought Oliver.

Plodding is slow and steady.

Plodding is reliable and honest.

Plodding gets you across deserts.

You don't see plodders being flashy smartypants.

Plodders don't think they can have everything.

If you find yourself investing your life savings in something called a collateralised debt obligation, which turns out to be four trillion dollars' worth of junk, you can be pretty sure it wasn't invented by a plodder.

I think plodding's good, thought Oliver.

There should be more of it.

If I survive this, from now on I'm going to be a plodder.

And proud of it.


And then even plodding got too difficult.

The water had been gone for hours, Nancy and Barclay were asleep on the float, Rose was stumbling like a zombie and Oliver knew he had about six more plods in him before he fell face down onto the desert and that was it.

One.

Two.

Three.

Four.

'Oliver,' croaked Nancy.

Oliver was so startled he almost fell over on four. It was ages since any of them had spoken.

He squinted at Nancy.

With a weary movement of her arm, she gestured to him to walk closer to the float.

Which, stumbling, he did.

'Oliver,' she whispered. 'There's something I have to say to you. About what I did with Barclay . . . what I threatened to do . . .'

She was having trouble getting the words out. Her lips were cracked and dusty.

'I'm sorry I did that,' she wheezed. 'Very sorry.'

She reached out and held his hand.

Oliver wanted to tell her it didn't matter now, they didn't have to talk about it now, it was better for her to save her energy.

He tried to tell her, but his mouth was too dry.

And then he realised why she was struggling to say all this now. It was in case there wasn't a chance later. In case they didn't make it.

'Don't,' he croaked. 'You don't have to . . .'

He tried to find the words to help her feel better, to let her know he understood, to tell her there would be a chance later. But he couldn't.

Suddenly Moo roared.

It was such a loud noise that Oliver almost stumbled again.

Rose was immediately alert. Nancy struggled to sit up. Barclay barked.

And then, from far away, Oliver heard a faint roaring in reply.

'Mum,' croaked Rose. 'Look.'

They stopped. Oliver looked. They were at the top of a slight ridge and there, below them in the distance, was a wooden house with a wide verandah and several smaller buildings around it.

Near the house was a fenced paddock.

In the paddock were camels, tiny, roaring.

Moo roared back.

'They're OK,' whispered Rose. 'Mum, they're still alive.'

Nancy didn't reply, and Oliver saw it was because she was having too many emotions.

He peered back down at the farm to make sure the camels were all on their feet, that none of them were slumped against the others or had fallen over.

Then Oliver saw something that gave him a lot of emotions too.

Parked near the house was Mum and Dad's car.

Next to it was a police car.

# 25

Moo led them down the slope at a trot.

Oliver hung onto the rope with Rose and tried to slow Moo down. Partly so the float didn't tip over and injure Nancy more, partly so he could try to work out why the police were at the farm.

To arrest Mum and Dad for bank crimes?

To arrest Nancy for kidnapping?

To arrest him for conspiracy to burgle and spying and demanding money by text?

As the float got closer to the farm, Oliver squinted desperately, trying to see Mum and Dad. They weren't in the open area between the house and the paddock.

Perhaps they were inside the house, or having a snooze in the car.

Oliver hoped so.

He hoped they weren't in the back of the police car with handcuffs on.

'Is that your parents' car?' said Rose.

Oliver nodded.

Rose's eyes narrowed. She didn't say anything. Oliver could tell from her scowl she was probably hoping Mum and Dad were not only in handcuffs, but chains as well.

Then he saw what she was actually scowling at.

Two police officers were running up the hill towards the float.

Nancy was half-sitting up and watching them anxiously. Oliver could see she was as worried as he was.

'Oliver,' she croaked. 'If they arrest me for anything, threatening an animal with a knife or neglecting camels or anything, Rose wasn't involved, OK? Will you tell them that?'

Rose glared at Oliver.

'You stay out of it,' she hissed at him. 'I'm telling them the whole thing was my fault.'

While Nancy and Rose argued in whispers, Oliver tried to stop the float, to turn it round so Nancy and Rose could get away. But it was hopeless, the float was too heavy and it was moving too fast behind Moo and . . .

One of the police officers grabbed Moo's rope and slowed her down.

The other one grabbed the float and slowed it down too.

'Jeez,' said the female officer. 'Good to see you lot. We were just about to get a search party out for you.'

169

'You look like you could do with a drink,' said the male officer. He held out a police water bottle. 'Sorry, you'll have to make do with this, the beer's run out.'

Nancy flopped back onto the swags. For a moment Oliver thought she'd fainted, but then he saw it was just relief.

Everyone had a drink.

Even Moo.

Oliver felt the water cooling him and making his thoughts clearer.

There were a million questions he wanted to ask, but only one of them was really important.

Where were Mum and Dad?

He didn't dare ask in case Mum and Dad hadn't been caught yet. In case they were hiding, and still free.

Now Oliver was closer to the farm he could see they weren't in either of the cars. And they hadn't come out of the house.

Where were they?

Oliver didn't see them until he and the others had almost reached the farm. Nancy grabbed his arm and silently pointed to a small hill a distance away on the other side of the house.

Oliver squinted.

And saw two figures standing on the hillside with their backs to him. It was definitely Mum and Dad, he recognised Mum's gold scarf.

He hoped the police officers hadn't seen them, but they had.

'They're the ones who called us,' said the male officer. 'They were worried about where you all were.'

Oliver felt weak with relief. No arresting seemed to be taking place. But why were Mum and Dad standing up there on the hillside?

They haven't even seen us, thought Oliver.

Mum and Dad were standing really still, with their heads bowed.

Strange, thought Oliver. That's not like Mum and Dad.

Mum and Dad were the sort of people who never stopped moving. It was like they had too much energy and nowhere to put it.

Oliver wondered what was going on.

He wanted to run over to them and let them know he was here. But there was something about the way they were standing.

It was like a private moment.

Oliver glanced at Rose. She was just looking at them too. Not yelling at them or throwing things, just looking at them.

So was Nancy.

On Nancy's face was almost as much emotion as when she'd seen the camels were alive.

'It's Tim's grave,' she said.

# 26

When Mum and Dad finally did notice everyone, they ran down from the grave so fast Oliver was worried they'd hurt themselves.

All they wanted to do for ages was hug Oliver.

He let them.

'Oh, love,' said Mum when she finally let go of Oliver long enough to speak. 'We found your note and we thought you'd gone to Vickey's. She wasn't answering her phone so we asked Hayden to go and check you were there. He said you were.'

Oliver thought about this.

'I don't think Hayden likes you much any more,' he said.

Mum and Dad both looked uncomfortable.

'What about the text I sent?' said Oliver. 'Why didn't you answer?'

'We didn't get it,' said Mum. 'Not till after the email. We were in a hotel hiding from the media and we had our phones turned off. Reporters wouldn't stop ringing us and Dad thought it was best.'

Dad looked even more uncomfortable. And Oliver could see it wasn't just because he was wearing a business shirt.

'That was a bad decision,' said Dad. 'I'm not proud of that.'

Oliver was stunned. He'd never heard Dad say anything like that before.

'Thank goodness you let us know you were coming here,' said Mum.

She hugged Oliver again.

Oliver glanced over at the paddock. Nancy was leaning against the fence watching Moo have a joyful reunion with the other camels. The police officers were helping Rose give the camels the last of the feed from the shed and the last of the water from the storage tank.

'Let's go onto the verandah,' said Oliver.

He led Mum and Dad over to the verandah, where they were further away from the police officers.

'I thought you could hide here at the farm,' said Oliver to Mum and Dad. 'I thought we could change our names and the police would never find us. So you wouldn't have to go to jail. But the police haven't even recognised you.'

Mum and Dad looked at him.

'Ollie,' said Dad, 'we're not going to jail. We're not even going to be arrested. Those news stories were just threats, to try to scare us into handing over our assets.'

'We didn't come here to hide,' said Mum. 'We came because we love you.'

Oliver's heart felt like a doggy tail that was thumping delightedly against his ribs.

Hang on, a doggy tail *was* thumping against his ribs.

Oliver turned. Barclay was on the verandah rail behind him, wagging excitedly and showing Oliver how delighted he was that everyone was here.

'This is Barclay,' said Oliver to Mum and Dad. 'He's my dog. Mine and Rose's.'

Mum and Dad took it well.

Which, Oliver thought, is the big advantage of losing all your priceless oriental rugs. It frees you up to like dogs.

Oliver pointed towards the paddock.

'That's Nancy and Rose,' he said.

Mum and Dad looked and nodded slowly.

Oliver could see they were both very nervous about saying hello to Nancy and Rose.

But they did, and after a few awkward moments, everyone relaxed a bit. Though Oliver saw Rose doing a fair bit of muttering.

The police officers explained they couldn't stay for dinner because they had a ninety-k drive back to the station, plus they had their own sandwiches.

After they'd gone, Oliver helped Rose set out

dinner on the verandah table. Mum and Dad had brought smoked salmon and an artichoke salad.

'Very kind,' said Nancy from her recliner lounge. 'Good tucker for a pair of bankrupts.'

Mum and Dad pretended to be busy with something else in their chill box.

'I'm having sardines from the cupboard,' muttered Rose, going into the kitchen.

Oliver understood.

'If you want to stay the night,' Nancy said to Mum and Dad, 'you'll have to bunk down on the floor because we had to sell the spare beds.'

Oliver saw Mum and Dad exchange a glance.

Come on, thought Oliver, how much of a hint do you need?

Dad cleared his throat.

'Before we eat,' he said, 'we have something for you.'

He handed Nancy a bulging envelope.

At last, thought Oliver.

Except the envelope didn't look big enough. Oliver had never actually seen a million dollars in money, but he was pretty sure it would need a suitcase.

'It's twenty-three thousand dollars,' said Dad to Nancy. 'Roughly what your investment would have paid you if it had gone as planned. We're sorry it didn't, Nancy, for your sake and for your family's sake.'

'Deeply sorry,' said Mum.

She reached over and squeezed Nancy's hand, and Oliver could see Mum was close to tears.

Except, if they were that sorry, where was the other nine hundred and something thousand?

'Thank you,' said Nancy. 'Now we've seen what you bankers have done to the world with your gambling dressed up as big business, I know I'm lucky to get it, and I'm grateful. And don't try giving me the other nine hundred and seventy-seven thousand, because I won't accept it.'

She glanced at Oliver, and Oliver was almost certain she gave him a wink. Then she stared up at the hillside for a while.

'I want to say sorry too,' she said finally to Mum and Dad. 'I did some things I'm not proud of. Ask Oliver. But I did them for my family.'

'Amen to that,' said Dad.

Oliver had a horrible feeling Dad was going to launch into a speech about how everything he'd done was for his family, including leaving his bank customers penniless.

Mum must have feared that as well, because she hastily interrupted.

'What are your plans now, Nancy?'

Nancy stared at the envelope.

'We'll try and make a go of it here,' she said. 'And if we can't, me and Rose will take a trip.'

'Somewhere nice?' said Dad. 'Bali or somewhere?'

Nancy shook her head.

'A big trip,' she said. 'If things don't work out

here, we'll walk the camels over to a friend of mine's property in Western Australia.'

Dad stared at her. So did Oliver.

'Wow,' said Dad. 'Across the desert?'

'No,' said Rose, coming out from the kitchen. 'We're gunna swim round the coast.'

'Rose,' said Nancy. 'Manners.'

Rose muttered something that didn't sound like sorry to Oliver.

'Yep,' said Nancy to Dad. 'Across the desert.'

'That must be, what, two thousand kilometres?' said Dad.

'Two and a half,' said Nancy. 'Take about six months.'

Oliver saw that Dad's eyes were shining.

'What an adventure,' said Dad. 'If you pulled off a trip like that, they'd be talking about you for years. They'd be talking about you in New York.'

Oliver sighed.

He leaned back in his chair and gazed up at the night sky.

Squillions of stars, every one an opportunity waiting to be grabbed, that's what Dad used to say when Oliver was little.

Mum used to say something different. Every star was there, she'd say, to shed light on a little step forward in life.

'I'd definitely be up for an adventure like that,' Dad was saying to Nancy. 'If we didn't have to go to Europe to start a new bank.'

It took Oliver a moment to realise what Dad had said.

He stared at Dad in horror.

A new bank?

Oliver had a vision of everything bad that had happened. He saw it all happening again. Only worse. And in Europe, where he wouldn't even be able to understand the housekeepers. And where he wouldn't see Barclay or Rose, or Moo or Nancy.

Ever.

Mum was staring at Dad too.

Oliver hoped she was horrified as well, but she wasn't.

She just looked very sad.

# 27

After dinner, Oliver found Mum in the paddock, standing in the moonlight, stroking Moo and some of the other camels.

'Hello, love,' she said. 'Amazing animals, aren't they? I still can't get over how Moo got you all here safely.'

'She was incredible,' said Oliver. 'She just kept plodding. She's really good at little steps forward in life.'

While Mum thought about that, Oliver stepped closer to Moo and put his cheek against Moo's face.

'Thank you,' he whispered. 'I'll never forget you.'

Moo's big puddle eyes glowed.

Oliver turned back to Mum, who was smiling sadly.

'Plodding,' she said. 'I like that. I wish I'd done a bit more plodding in my life.'

Oliver took a deep breath.

'Mum,' he said. 'Do you want to go to Europe?'

Mum stared at the camels for a while.

She shook her head.

'What I wish,' she said, 'is that we could make a new start. As a family. The three of us together. But it's not going to happen, not while your father has money to play with. Which is why I sometimes wish me and Dad had lost everything.'

Oliver stared at her.

'Not completely everything,' said Mum. 'We've got to live. But almost everything.'

She put her arm round Oliver and went back to gazing at the camels.

After a while, Oliver kissed Mum on the cheek and told her he was going to say goodbye to Rose and Barclay.

'Don't stay up too late,' said Mum. 'We have to leave very early in the morning to get to the airport.'

'I won't,' said Oliver.

He meant it. He was feeling too tired for a late night. And too sad.

Rose was in the feed shed, sweeping up the last wisps of camel feed.

She looked at Oliver as he came in. She didn't smile, but at least she didn't mutter anything.

In the dusty haze of the shed, lit by a single bare light globe, Oliver had the crazy thought that her hair looked even more like camel feed than camel feed.

Barclay came bounding over from sniffing a rat hole and jumped into Oliver's arms.

Rose looked at them.

'Thanks for lending me Barclay,' she said.

Oliver looked at her, puzzled.

Didn't she understand?

Barclay was hers now.

'You were kind,' said Rose. 'But he's yours. You need him more than I do.'

Oliver wondered if camel-feed dust could muddle a person's thinking.

'I'm going to Europe tomorrow,' he said miserably. 'I can't take a dog.'

Barclay started licking Oliver's face.

Oliver wished Barclay would stop. Any more of this and he'd be crying in front of a girl. Which he didn't want to do, not even a special girl like Rose.

'Do you want to go to Europe?' said Rose. 'Do you want to hang out in some flash joint over there?'

Oliver shook his head.

'Then do something about it,' she said.

They looked at each other.

'Sometimes,' said Rose, 'you lose things and you can't do anything about it. But sometimes you can.'

Oliver thought about what it would be like to live in a normal house with a normal garden. A garden with Barclay in it. And a spare bedroom so Rose could come and visit. Or even just a pull-out sofa.

He also thought about what it would be like to walk to Western Australia with Rose and Nancy and the camels and Barclay and Mum and Dad.

One day.

Maybe.

And suddenly Oliver knew exactly what he could do.

For a moment he had trouble speaking.

'Thanks,' he said finally.

He wanted to give Rose a grateful hug, but without any injured camels around he thought that might be pushing it for now.

# 28

Even after his late night, Oliver got up early with everyone else.

While Mum and Dad took the bags to the car, and discovered they had four punctures, Oliver waited on the verandah with Nancy.

'Desert roads,' Nancy called to Mum and Dad from her recliner. 'Murder on city tyres. You'll find a repair kit in the kitchen dresser.'

Dad swore for a while, then went inside.

Oliver tried not to look guilty.

Nancy's face, he saw, was completely free of all guilt. And the big kitchen knife was out of sight under her recliner.

'You'd better go and see Brendan now,' Nancy said to Oliver, pointing.

Rose and Barclay were over by the water-storage tank. Rose was giving money to the driver of a water truck, which had a trailer behind it stacked with camel feed.

'He's a quick unloader, is Brendan,' said Nancy.

Oliver hurried over to the water truck. This bit he didn't feel guilty about at all.

Brendan had already started winding the hose back onto the truck. Rose glanced at Oliver, then carried a bale of feed into the shed.

'Excuse me, Brendan,' said Oliver. 'Could you post a letter for me?'

He took an envelope from his back pocket and held it out to Brendan.

Brendan took it and looked at the address.

'Canberra,' he said. 'Australian Securities and Investment Commission. Is it important?'

Oliver decided to be completely honest.

It was what Nancy and Rose had advised him to do when they helped him print the photo late last night. Tell Brendan the truth so he wouldn't think this was some kind of kid's prank.

'It's a bank statement,' said Oliver. 'From a Swiss bank account that belongs to my parents. I'm sending it to the authorities so the customers of my parents' failed investment bank can get some of their money back.'

Brendan looked at the envelope.

He nodded gravely.

'Important then,' he said. 'I'll make sure it gets off today.'

When Oliver went back to the verandah, Nancy gave him a nod. Well done, the nod said.

A black-and-white streak, yelping with joy, hurtled across from the water tank and leaped onto Oliver's chest and wagged mud all over him and made his face wet with love.

Oliver hugged Barclay for a moment.

Then, cheeks still wet, he looked across at the shed. Rose was standing in the doorway, watching him. She gave him a grin and a thumbs up.

Oliver grinned back.

There wasn't anything he wanted more than this.

OK, one thing.

The thing he had to do now.

Show Mum and Dad that if you're prepared to take the right sort of risk, the world can be a sweet and perfect place.

Oliver took a deep breath and walked over to tell Mum her wish had come true.

*Morris Gleitzman's three remarkable books about children in the Holocaust . . .*

My name is Felix

Once I saved a girl called Zelda from a burning house

I had a plan for both of us

Pretend to be someone else

Be safe forever

Then the Nazis came